THE PREMISE, THE MONEY & THE GOLD

CHRISTOPHER ANZALONE
With Dennis Ross III

The Premise, The Money and The Gold is a work of fiction. Names, characters, places, and incidents either are the products of the author's imagination or are used fictitiously. Any resemblance to actual persons, living or dead, events, or locales is entirely coincidental.

Copyright © 2012 Christopher Anzalone and Dennis Ross, III and Write Investment Books, Atlanta, Georgia

All rights reserved.

No part of this publication may be reproduced, distributed, or transmitted in any form or by any means, including photocopying, recording, or other electronic or mechanical methods, without the prior written permission of the publisher, except in the case of brief quotations embodied in critical reviews and certain other noncommercial uses permitted by copyright law.

Library of Congress Cataloging-in-Publication Data

Ordering Information: Quantity sales and special discounts are available on bulk purchases by corporations, professional associations, academic institutions and others. For details, contact dross@writeinvestment.com

Printed in the United States of America

Design: Sergio Velez

Photo: Kate Benson

ISBN 978-0-615-66991-5

For Danielle, my rare diamond

CONTENTS

Introduction..5

Chapter 1. THE PREMISE....................................9

Chapter 2. THE DOCTOR..................................21

Chapter 3. THE CONFERENCE.........................35

Chapter 4. THE TRANSCRIPT...........................55

Chapter 5. THE CODE.......................................71

Chapter 6. THE HISTORY OF MONEY.............95

Chapter 7. THE BANK.....................................109

Chapter 8. THE INFORMATION.....................127

Chapter 9. THE CONFRONTATION...............147

Chapter 10. THE FUTURE OF MONEY..........163

Chapter 11. THE LOSING GAME....................175

Acknowledgments..189

INTRODUCTION

A STRAIGHT LINE IS ONLY EFFICIENT when you're headed in the right direction. Otherwise, you simply get to the wrong destination faster.

This thought gives birth to a question. Who is providing the information on which you base your decisions, especially your investment decisions? Further, how vigorous are you in ensuring the information you're given isn't biased towards what ultimately benefits the source of the information? And if you found out the information was either incorrect or incomplete, what would you do to change course?

The paradox of making the right investment decisions is you must first make the wrong ones. Yes, you must. Financial wisdom operates on the purest principle of tough love - no one gets off the hook, no one skates free. All investors pay tuition in the form of losses. But how much tuition you pay is up to you. The amount of your 'tuition' will directly depend on your exposure to, acceptance of, and implementation of better information, which also happens to be unpopular information.

You've probably noticed how becoming wealthy and staying wealthy are two very different skill sets. But one trait is common to both; you must think properly. And thinking properly requires clarity; one cannot process mud. Most financial advice given to the general public is mud. Most financial advice is opinion assertively spoken in a manner that is intentionally complex. Complexity is the greatest disguise for incompetence.

***

The best way to see the problem with traditional investment advice is to step away from the subject of investment advice entirely, and to instead focus the lens from a distance. If the advice you're receiving would not work in any other area outside of your money, it is bad advice. Solid principles are solid within any framework. Gravity doesn't care who jumps off the roof; it still works.

This book is a unique presentation on how to recognize and apply more solid principles in all areas of our lives – but it's more than that. It's about how we routinely make bad decisions, not based on fallacy, but rather on authoritative information. And why it is precisely that, in the presence of authoritative data, we must be on our greatest guard to avoid the peripheral decisions that grow from false nucleus. Peripheral decisions are best described as the second generation of bad premise. Peripheral decisions are more potent than their fallacious origin because they are stronger, more elegant and more nuanced, like a traveling flu resistant to antibiotics. Peripheral decisions often determine our fate and the fate of those we love - forever. It's not the mistake that gets you; it's the mistake that follows the mistake.

***

All decisions are fundamentally based on premise. In the world of philosophy, premise is sometimes expressed

INTRODUCTION

as *blik* (pronounced *blick*). Your blik is your mental starting point, and it is rarely, if ever, reviewed. If the world is an oil painting, your blik is the frame. Your blik encases everything inside of it. It holds certain ideas together, while rejecting others. Your blik defines your personal standards of evidence. For example, a man with a paranoid frame or blik processes all events as hostile, regardless of their true intent. He sees conspiracy even in kindness. A simple smile from a stranger is but another diabolical distraction – an attempt to trick him into relaxing so he can be attacked. The man with a dogmatic religious frame sees God in everything around him. The sun and moon aren't nature, but rather evidence of his premise of the creator/creation relationship. But before you paint these persons as illogical for their beliefs, think of this:

The average investor operates under a blik called Wall Street. This "Wall Street blik" causes an investor to see evidence for a good investment where there is none. Wall Street bliks cause investors to grant credit to 'independent' research that is everything but. These bliks keep people from doing their own research, or even asking their own questions. The Wall Street blik convinces the general public to ignore their gut when it comes to their money, even though their gut has never led them wrong before. Thankfully, all of this can be overcome.

The challenge is that valuable information is often presented to us by people outside our standards of evidence. Thus, we degrade the information before it has an opportunity to benefit our lives. But better information and a better process is within your reach.

What if a homeless man wrote you a $1 million dollar check on a bank you'd never heard of? What would be your first reaction? Like most people, you would probably be skeptical of its validity because you have no legitimate frame of reference for the check. After all, a homeless man doesn't have $1 million dollars to give you.

Now using this same example, what if a Wall Street giant handed you a $1 million dollar check written on a well-known bank in the US? Because of who gave you the check, you would probably be overwhelmed with joy because your *blik* provides comfort in knowing that Wall Street giants have money.

Now what if I told you the homeless man's name was Howard Hughes and the Wall Street giant was Bernie Madoff? Notice that without knowing the names of the individuals giving the checks, you simply credited or discredited the giver, based on their position in life.

Readers of this book will soon realize why the greatest innovation is not technology; it is innovation of the mind. It is the repositioning of previously held assumptions in order to make sure your conclusions are based on fact, because so much is at stake.

Welcome to *The Premise, The Money and The Gold*.

Chapter One
THE PREMISE

CHAPTER ONE: THE PREMISE

"YOU HAVE ONE NEW MESSAGE," the computerized voice announced from the speakerphone. "Stan, Barry here - got your message. I really think you should reconsider. Gold is just way too speculative. It's for cowboys. We have a conservative, more thoughtful game plan. I know we're down pretty big right now - but everybody is. The market is coming back, it always does." Hearing this, Jesse began tiptoeing down the stairs.

"Look, we have a new research guy who has some great insights into gold ETFs."

Jessica slipped under the curtains without disturbing their position.

"If you want gold exposure, then ETFs are the way to go. I mean - it's your call, but buying physical gold, physical bullion just isn't smart for many reasons. Anyway, we'll talk more - call when you get a chance."

Jessica was now pressed against the worn leather couch; she peeked around its edge.

As usual, Stanley hadn't heard her. He was contemplating what he'd just heard from his financial advisor -another dismissal of his investment ideas.

All Jessica had to do now was negotiate that one squeaky spot in the floor. Like a spider, she stretched her right foot, balanced herself, and easily avoided the area sure to blow her cover.

And out of nowhere, a beautiful innocence filled the air in a way only five year-olds can produce.

*"Happy birthday to you, happy birthday to you,
Happy bi-r-r-rth day dear daddy, happy birthday to you!"*

Stanley swiveled his chair toward the melody. His eyes now closed but filled with tears. With his arms opened wide, he called out.

"Jessica, is that you?"

"It's me, daddy - happy birthday."

"Come here, Jesse!"

She leapt to her feet and ran into her father's arms.

"Who put you up to this? You're like a little spider. You're always hiding in here."

She frowned, taking her daddy too seriously.

"I'm not a spider."

A name given to her for the countless times Stanley found her hiding under the couch while he was working.

"I know sweetheart - you're my little princess - I love you."

"Love you too, daddy."

"Go tell your mom I'm headed up for dinner."

Little Jesse jumped down and then paused.

"Daddy, I want to be just like you," she said and ran upstairs, her purple slippers disappearing around the corner.

Stanley let out a long, deep breath. His life was full, his family precious, but he was still disturbed.

"There's got to be a better way," he thought to himself.

"Maybe I should put all this stuff down for now and just enjoy the day."

For the past three hours, he had been reading through brokerage statements. He was studying technical stock charts. He was reviewing his investments, all of which had taken a merciless beating.

It was 2008. The DOW was at 8,200 - the S & P was hovering around 690, and the NASDAQ had just touched 1380. Stanley's portfolio fell from $2 million in 2006 to

CHAPTER ONE: THE PREMISE

$800,000 today. What took him eighteen years to save was cut in half in eighteen months. But everywhere he turned, every person he spoke with made losing money sound so normal. His own research proved how several ideas he'd presented to his advisors over the years would have worked out much better. Stanley needed a retirement he could depend on. He needed an advisor who would listen. For him, financial stability equaled peace, and he was not peaceful. The little sign on his desk reads:

"If money can't make you happy, why does poverty make you sad?"

The floor above him creaked.

Stan grabbed his pen and put it back in its color-coordinated case, twisting the monogram such that all the pens faced twelve o'clock.

Knowing his wife well, in about three minutes, she would realize he hadn't gotten up and headed straight upstairs. But this investment thing had been bothering him for years, and thinking about it had him stuck in his seat on his birthday. Their 401k kept bleeding. He had suggested that his broker liquidate certain positions when he was down 30%; he asked again at 40% and at 60%, he was too upset to even call. He couldn't understand how this had happened, and why did he sit by and just watch? Yes, the markets were volatile and everyone had suffered in the past few years, but he had a nagging feeling that it didn't have to be this way.

He just didn't know how and where to go to change what was happening to his hard-earned money. To make things worse, the financial leakage in his portfolio was seemingly now on a fast track, so today, on his fiftieth birthday, he decided to review the brokerage statements he was so often told to simply file away.

His training as a mechanical engineer helped him create a robust spreadsheet. The data went far beyond cost basis, unrealized profit and loss, technical analysis and so forth. His data created a virtual, parallel portfolio showing how the investments he was advised against were doing in real time.

What he learned was unreal. Gold would have saved his backside. But every time he presented his research, his advisor would say, "Anybody can make money paper trading; leave investing to the pros." And so Stanley would put his ideas back in their little box. But things were about to change.

Stanley finally had the energy to turn his attention towards something other than his health. Staying healthy had been the primary focus for three years now. Along with following doctor's orders, he'd made practical adjustments to his lifestyle. Reducing red meat intake, and losing thirty pounds had done him good. He hadn't seen "190" on a bathroom scale since college. It felt good. And just like he had proactively concentrated on his health, it was now time to take control of the money he worked so hard to amass, the money that was now slipping through his grasp.

Five minutes had passed since little Jesse ran upstairs. Like a bowling ball, he heard the low rumble of his wife's footsteps crossing from one side of the house to the other. She was headed his way.

"Coming up now, honey!" Stan yelled at the staircase.

"Stanley?" Her voice signaled she didn't believe him.

He swiveled his chair, straightened the rug under his desk that had been disturbed when Jesse surprised him, and headed up.

CHAPTER ONE: THE PREMISE

"I'm here, honey," he said to his wife, Nicole, who was standing at the top of the stairs - her hands crossed in loving frustration.

"Stan – it's is your birthday, can we celebrate?"

***

"What were you thinking?" Nicole asked, the two of them lying in bed, reviewing the birthday party and laughing about Stanley's crazy uncle who came over for the party earlier in the day –the uncle who refuses to wear socks, even when he wears a suit and dress shoes. "Why would you tell him that you're thinking about buying gold? He didn't stop talking about it for thirty minutes straight!"

Nicole paused and launched into her best Uncle Joe impersonation, allowing her voice to grow deeper and more hoarse. "You can't buy beer with gold," she said. "You can't get your car fixed with gold, you can't do this; you can't do that."

"Very interesting – funny, but interesting." Stan replied. "If I didn't know any better, I'd think you agreed with him."

"Well, you *do* know better," Nicole responded, turning her attention to the real question. "So what is it? What are you so worried about?"

"Just thinking about our finances," he answered vaguely.

"Stan, you promised not to . . ."

"I know," Stan said. "I've done what I promised. I promised to concentrate on my health. That's gotten better now and I think it's time to refocus my efforts on our retirement. Since 2006, our 401k has lost 60% in value. Our $2,000,000 is now $800,000. I'm an engineer, Nicole. I design things that work, or that at least have a high probability of working in most environments. I'm beginning to think the

15

investment advice we've been given simply isn't working. Anybody can lose money, but the pros are supposed to make a difference. Otherwise, why do we pay them?"

"Everyone is losing right now," Nicole said.

"Wow, you sound like Barry." Stan responded.

"Are we supposed to feel better because financial suffering is widespread? Imagine your doctor saying, 'we gotta take your leg off but don't worry, lots of folks don't have legs these days.' It's crazy, terribly flawed logic. A cop out for incompetence in my opinion."

"So what exactly do you suggest?" she asked.

Stan sighed. This was what he'd been waiting for, though he hadn't realized it until now. He and Nicole had been married for ten years, and she was his best friend. He valued her thoughts over anyone else's. Now she was offering to brainstorm with him. It was some of the best news he'd heard in a long time.

"What I *think*," he said with satisfaction, "is that there has to be a better way. If the doctor told me he was going to cut off my leg, I'd listen to him and respect what he had to say, sure. But I sure as hell wouldn't go into the operation without doing research and getting a second opinion! I'd want to find out as much as I could before I made any decision!"

"Okay, that makes sense," Nicole conceded, "And?"

"And the same should apply to our money! We've spent years doing what Barry said we should do, without question. We never bothered to do our own research. Getting a second opinion; I think that's where we went wrong."

"You think we should be asking more questions, making more of our own decisions," she murmured, repeating his train of thought.

"Yes, exactly! I've taken suggestions to Barry before, but he always discounts them. He puts my ideas on sale for half

CHAPTER ONE: THE PREMISE

price. I ran the numbers today. I built one of those spreadsheets - turns out I was right. If we'd done what I thought we should have, we'd be better off. Way better off."

"How much better, exactly?"

"We would have lost maybe 10% to everyone else's 60%."

Nicole forced air through her teeth, making a soft, high-pitched whistle. "Our retirement funds would still be there?"

"Yep." Stan answered.

"If I'd stood my ground, if I'd been firmer with Barry, I could have held onto all that money for us. But I gave in because he was supposed to be the expert. He was supposed to be the one who knew what he was talking about. I blew off my gut feelings to take some very, very bad advice."

"Mmhmm," Nicole answered softly, allowing a touch of sarcasm to enter her voice. "And what is it that would have saved our money exactly?"

"Gold, Nikki," Stan answered. "It's that simple. If we'd been in gold, we would have been Ok."

Nicole was silent for a moment, thinking about what he'd said. "So what are you going to do about it, now?" she asked finally.

"Well, I'll give you the short version. I'm going to stop doing everything Barry tells me to do, I'll tell you that much. I'm going to start doing more research – a *lot* more research, about gold, silver, other precious metals. And I'm going to see where we can go with it. I'm going to start listening to my gut, plain and simple."

"Well, I'll back you up as much as I can, you know that. And speaking of your gut, you have that appointment with your doctor tomorrow. Go get your test results; then come home. I'll have dinner ready. We'll open a bottle of wine

17

and get to work, figure out what needs to change, and how we're going to do it, deal?"

"Deal."

Stan got up and turned off all the lights in the house; he made sure all blinds were closed at a ninety degree angle - a habit he formed ever since studying the blind spots of the human eye. Climbing back into bed, he had one more thought.

"You know, I'm almost embarrassed to say this but I don't even know who Barry is, why we hired him in the first place or what he's ever done. I do more investigative shopping in the produce isle of the grocery store when I'm tapping on melons. How did that happen?"

Nicole could only fake a smile.

"I mean - think about it. We shopped for six months for a new car, compared loans against loans, dealership against dealership and then we test drove cars until that new car smell made us vomit. We did all the research, asked all the right questions, and thought for ourselves instead of doing what the first salesman told us we should do. But we handed our life's earnings to a guy who's been losing money in stocks from day one, and then stayed with him throughout. Unreal, just unreal."

"It does seem a bit idiotic, when you put it that way," Nicole answered. "I guess it just didn't occur to us to question it."

"Right, that's exactly it – we were sheep in a herd, ants to a picnic. Everyone else does what their financial advisor suggests, so who were we to question it? He was so confident that we just kept listening to him."

Nicole sighed, "Well, we know better now, and that's what counts."

"Oh, I know better now alright," Stan said firmly. He

CHAPTER ONE: THE PREMISE

could feel himself starting to get fired up about it, but couldn't seem to stop. He'd been frustrated about this situation for a long time, but had kept his thoughts inside, until now.

"I'm going to take things into my own hands, tell *them* where I want my money to go and why. And I'm not going to take 'no' for an answer. I'm going to start asking questions, damm it! And getting answers! And the first question I'm going to ask is; 'Why weren't you listening when I presented my ideas about gold years ago?' I don't understand why on earth everyone is trying to keep us away from gold?"

As if providing an escape, Nicole placed her index finger over Stan's mouth,

"Go to sleep."

Chapter Two
THE DOCTOR

CHAPTER TWO: THE DOCTOR

STAN LOOKED AT HIS WATCH. Twelve noon. It would take him exactly twenty-eight minutes to drive to the doctor's office. He paid the check and aimed for the door at Keso, his favorite Mexican spot. The food was good, but the people were great. He hadn't walked five steps before turning around and heading back to the cashier. The floor was tiled; Stan made sure he didn't step on any lines. He was funny like that. The simplest things bothered him while other, more serious, consequential events could slip under his nose undetected.

"Beautiful shirt." Stan told the pretty young cashier with cleavage so strategically placed as to be mathematical.

She smiled, thinking he'd reversed his trajectory to pay her a forgotten comment – when in reality he was padding the trivial request to come.

"May I see that receipt again?" He asked. Surprised, she grabbed the stack of receipts finding his on top. With his pen, Stan retraced his signature; one small area didn't fill in correctly.

"You didn't have to do that sir," the cashier said, smiling, the kind of smile that points to disappointment.

"Actually, I did," Stan replied.

As an outgrowth of his Boeing engineering work, Stan viewed life as an elegantly interconnected organism. In his thinking, anything left incomplete affects the integrity of all events to come. Stan was always looking to close the circle. He was always looking to protect future events against random risk. After all, he's responsible for keeping planes in the sky. His professional and academic experience deeply ingrained in him one fact - the tiniest overlooked item can be the first step towards catastrophe. Assumptions can be deadly.

But it was the one area of finance that ran untamed in his life. He'd never applied skills of critical logic to his money.

It was the one area he'd turned over to the 'experts.' Stan knew engineering, but he didn't know finance, and so he trusted those who did. Ironically, this approach was logical to him. As an engineer, companies hired him to do what they knew needed to be done but didn't have the experience to do. Why should money management be any different? Shouldn't you always go with the experts?

***

Making sure his tires triggered the crosswalk sign, Stan came to a full stop at the first red light after leaving Keso. A little girl walking across with her mother reminded him of Jesse. She waved and wouldn't look away.

Stan waved back, immediately feeling a pain. He grabbed his chest, twisting it to squeeze out the pain.

The girl's smile turned into concern as she watched Stan from over her left shoulder.

He'd had the same pain for a few weeks now; even taking his medicine on time each day, the pain hadn't stopped. His primary doctor referred him to a specialist and today, Tuesday, was the day to see her again, Dr. Angelo – the best around. Stan needed to make sure his condition had not returned after so many years.

***

The Examination Room

With his back now arched – Stan moved to the edge of the table. He could hear the doctor's footsteps closing in, his results in her hand. But her stride sounded hesitant.

CHAPTER TWO: THE DOCTOR

"Maybe she's preoccupied or reading another chart while walking towards my room– no biggie. I'm just overly observant," he jokingly thought to himself.

The doctor's shadow made it to the door before she did. Her white shoe planted in the doorway as the other pivoted to answer a question yelled from behind her.

"I need twenty minutes," she yelled back.

"Twenty minutes to give me my results?" Stan thought.

Making no eye contact, Dr. Angelo placed her clipboard on the sink top.

That's weird; she made eye contact immediately during the last visit, he thought. An odd feeling - but maybe it's nothing.

The atmosphere in the room was becoming increasingly still, only adding to Stan's uneasiness. The more anxious he was, the slower his mind worked, everything at half speed. His tendency to notice everything kicked in.

"These florescent lights are really bright - I wonder how the guy who empties those toxic needles keeps from being stuck day after day?" Random observations jumped into his mind.

Dr. Angelo grabbed the chair near the door and dragged it across the floor. The sound was loud and abrasive. She sat down and smiled in the most professional way possible.

The only time people are this professional is to counterbalance a looming emotion, Stan thought. *Exactly seventeen seconds have gone by and she's yet to say a word.* He snapped a mental photo of everything: seven buttons on the doctor's jacket, button number six hanging by its own thread; her jacket pure white, except for one spot, which seemed to be faded blood – and her hands. Her nails were freshly done, but her mascara an hour past needing retouching. When she sat down, a whiff of her scent hinted of ovulation.

Where's my head? Stan thought. *What am I thinking about?*

"Hi, doctor!" he rushed into verbal conversation to silence the inappropriate randomness of his thoughts.

"We need to talk," Dr. Angelo said.

Three hard knocks shook the room.

"Doctor?" her long-time nurse and confidant, Gozi, called from the hall and stuck her head into the doorway before hearing an answer. Dr. Angelo looked up in mild surprise that her discussion with Stan had been so interrupted.

"Mary Stein; room three, blood pressure has dropped to eighty over fifty in just the last few minutes."

"Call 911," The doctor said calmly as she raced towards the door, leaving her papers face down on the seat.

Stanley could hear the commotion in the next room as an older man's voice kept asking, "Mary? Mary?"

I hope she's gonna be ok, Stan thought, overhearing the increasing commotion.

He kept looking at those papers on the seat.

Stan wanted to turn them over and see what the doctor needed to speak to him about. He looked at the door left open when Dr. Angelo ran out. He looked back at the papers. He got up and walked towards the door to close it so he could quickly scan the notes. He touched the papers and immediately felt vibration in his back pocket.

"What the?" his cell phone was ringing. It felt as if God was slapping the back of his hand. Caller ID said 'Jesse and Nicole.' Whenever Nicole called, she always put Jesse on first. Stan placed the papers back on the chair face down and answered.

"Hey, princess."

CHAPTER TWO: THE DOCTOR

"Hi dad – here's mom,"

"Hi honey - just calling to see how everything is going."

"Things are fine," Stan answered. "Waiting on the doctor to come back in. We were talking and another patient had a little emergency so now I'm back waiting again.

"Ok, just give me a call when you leave and tell me how it went.

"Will do - bye."

Stan walked back to the door and cracked it open to see how far the doctor was away to gage how much time he had to read her notes; he saw her coat turn the corner down the hall. He swung the door back to its original position and rushed back to his table, jumping up onto the edge in the same position he was in when she left.

Dr. Angelo walked in as somberly the second time as she did the first. She sat down.

"Stan, your biopsy came back malignant, but we are unable to operate."

Silence.

"What are you talking about?" His stature crumbled. "But I thought we were past the period of concern?"

"Stan, it's come back, you need to…"

Stan interrupted. His voice shaking badly, sweat sharpening the tips of his hair. "Doctor, the same lab that said it was gone is now saying it's back?"

"Stan – it is back."

"Based on what premise?"

"Science," said Dr. Angelo.

"Well, what I mean is, how do I know – well, how do we know the report is right? I mean – couldn't they be wrong at least sometimes?"

"Stan, of all the things we don't know in this world, medical science isn't at the top of the list. Denial is normal, and expected – for awhile, but you need to go home and speak to Nicole."

"Jesse is three."

His eyes caught the clock on the wall. 1:37pm. Stress had turned his face beet red. He straightened his back and scooted back to the table's edge - leaned forward and whispered in terms only a parent could understand.

"She's three, doctor."

Dr. Angelo responded in the same sentiment of her earlier advice.

"You need to spend time with your family, you need to travel. You need to get your house in order."

Stan didn't receive Dr. Angelo's words in the same way they were sent.

"Get my house in order? Am I hearing you correctly?" he said, over-articulating each word. All conversations in adjacent rooms lowered as the rising emotion in his spread through the walls.

His hands now squeezing his forehead, Stan began to cry as in as manly a way as possible. The more he tried to control himself, the less control he had. All he could think about was Jesse.

"Dr. Angelo?" The voice called from the other side of the door.

"Is everything alright?" Gozi asked.

"Yes." The doctor answered.

Dr. Angelo stood up, washed her hands and picked up the clipboard.

"I will prescribe some medication to assist you with your pain as it will become more intense over the coming months."

CHAPTER TWO: THE DOCTOR

"Months?" Stan asked.

"Yes." The doctor answered.

"How - how long do I have?"

"Three to six months at the most." The doctor placed her right hand on his shoulder.

"Stanley, may God be with you strong." She turned and walked out the room, closing the door carefully behind her.

***

Stan tried desperately to gather himself. His phone rang.

'Nicole and Jesse.' Nicole calling back. He didn't answer this time, knowing she would call back almost immediately. He needed a few seconds to calm down enough so she wouldn't suspect anything. He rushed to the examining room sink, washed his face, blew his noise and gritted his teeth.

The phone rang again.

In the moments of waiting for his wife to call back, Stan decided that he couldn't tell her what he'd just heard. He simply could not, at least not now, tell his family only one day after his birthday that he wouldn't be around to see another one.

"Hi, honey! Stan, how's it going, what did the doctor say?"

"Tests were inconclusive, gonna run them again in a couple of weeks."

Pause.

"Oh – ok, so she didn't have any information at all?" Nicole asked.

"Not really; she said everything for right now is the same as it was until they do more tests, but I think everything is going to be ok."

"Good to know, I look forward to your next appointment," she said.

Silence.

"Alright, headed home to start working on our investments, speak soon."

Stan walked outside. It was a beautiful Tuesday in Austin. The sun seemed to pay no attention to the pain right beneath it. Stan could only concentrate on one thing. He wasn't going to be around to see little Jesse grow. He would miss her first bike ride, her first homework assignment. How could he possibly tell his family this?

Arriving home, he walked slowly up the sidewalk in front of his small white house, careful to avoid cracks in the pavement, counting each picket in his picket fence. Before entering, he peered through the front window. Nicole and Jesse were playing.

"How do I walk in there?" he thought.

Jesse saw him.

"There's daddy!" she pointed. He wasn't ready, but he must walk in now without hesitation.

"What did Dr. Angelo say?" Nicole asked with a forced cheerfulness.

Stan placed his bag on the kitchen floor and decided delay wasn't the proper strategy.

"It's back."

These words instantly stained Nicole's eyes with red, "What do you mean? They told us the worst was over!"

"I know. I don't know what happened..."

"So what does this mean? Are you going to have to change your medication or go on –"

"Inoperable. Dr. Angelo can't do anything." The air in the kitchen became humid, suffocating.

"Listen closely," Stan said. "Say nothing to Jesse. We're

CHAPTER TWO: THE DOCTOR

still going on vacation next month, still going to enjoy our time at the beach. We're still going to live life.

***

Privately, Stan had begun intense counseling sessions a year earlier. Few people knew he'd been clinically depressed. He'd started going to counseling to learn how to handle his obsessive behaviors, how to channel the secret anger he kept so hidden. The counseling helped some. He'd lost weight, and in many ways, tamed the demons. And just a few months earlier, when his lab tests had come back negative and he'd received a clean bill of health, Stan's positive outlook on life only increased. But now that bill of health had been pulled away, and he was falling back into the same depression, this time, only worse. There'd been at least a little bit of hope before – the idea of medication, surgery, even holistic treatments. This time he didn't have that. He had a death sentence. His condition today - inoperable and the medication, only good for reducing pain. Three to six months to live? It was more than his mind could process. He was sinking, and he wasn't sure what to do about it.

Shortly after receiving his diagnosis Stan started feeling physically better, but he wasn't supposed to. He was supposed to get weaker and weaker as the weeks passed. He decided to take a leave from Boeing. On the first day, he took his coffee straight into his home office and collapsed into his oversized button leather chair. He needed to think, and this was the best place. His desk was his resting place. This was the little spot on earth where he could make important decisions.

Stan walked to the top stair, closed the door he had left ajar and headed back to his desk. The clock said 1:30. With a little time on his hands, he thought he'd catch up on a few calls, unreturned since learning of his diagnosis. He called the lawn care company and asked them to lower his monthly rate as slow rain in Austin made their service nearly unnecessary. They agreed. His childhood friend, Anan Book, a black South African whose accent grew more aggressive and less understandable the more emotional he got, had left several messages for Stan over the past few days. Always the same message, "Stan, call me!"

Book had wanted to know if Stan planned to come to the class reunion. Stan had mixed feelings about going, but had to call his buddy back.

"I'll see if I can make it," he told Anan.

"Stan, don't you play wit me, you need to be der!" Anan said in his strong, barely intelligible accent.

"Ok – ok, I'll try," Stan answered. "Really great to hear from you, Anan."

"Wonderful speaking, Stan. See you soon."

They hung up at the same time without saying goodbye - a lifelong tradition between them – no goodbyes. It was 1:36. The gun was sitting on top of his counselor's business card.

I just don't think they understand how depressed I am, Stan thought to himself. He reached forward and entered the code to the top drawer – "One, nine, thirty-seven." The drawer popped open, he grabbed a loaded clip.

His hand began to shake.

It took him a few seconds to push the clip in – he couldn't seem to get the alignment right.

Stan looked up and saw his favorite photo – the one of Jesse and Santa when she was two. Reaching for it, he caressed his daughter's face and then gently laid the picture facedown. *She didn't need to see this.*

CHAPTER TWO: THE DOCTOR

The clock said 1:37. He racked the gun, closed his eyes tightly, and raised it to his forehead, putting a bit of pressure on the trigger as his eyes tightened, just a bit more and it would be over.

Suddenly, his back pocket vibrated; his cell phone. Stan had forgotten to turn it off.

"My God, can't a man commit suicide in peace?" he muttered. He yanked the phone out and reached for the 'ignore' button, when he recognized the phone number.

"It's my doctor."

Chapter Three
THE CONFERENCE

CHAPTER THREE: THE CONFERENCE

LANDING AT LAGUARDIA, GEORGE POWERED UP HIS PHONE. It would be at least fifteen minutes before passengers were allowed off the plane, but with the engines powered down, he could check his messages. The message light indicated a full inbox.

"That's odd," George thought. "I emptied all my messages before leaving Miami this morning. Probably the office."

George is an avid investor and successful business owner. Anytime he isn't running his fleet of automotive shops, he's reading a book on the markets. On the plane, he was reading about investing in gold, and the numbers were staggering - but confusing. He's been trying to invest in physical gold for years, but was constantly discouraged by the financial experts at the brokerage firm he used. He figured there must be something he didn't know because surely the firm would get him in gold if it would make him money. George was in New York to find out for himself. He needed to understand gold once and for all.

Sitting on the plane, George began listening to his voice mail.

"George, please call me when you get this message," his wife sounded calm - but concerned. He listened to the next message.

"George, hope this is your right number - this is the doctor's office. Please give us a call when you get a chance." The next message, and the next, and the next were from his wife. He hung up and called home.

"Carol, what's going on?"

"That's what I was wondering," she answered. "The doctor's office called twice and I wanted to know why."

"Let me call them and call you back."

"Angelo and Associates, how may I help you?"

"Yes - may I speak to Dr. Angelo's nurse?"

37

"One moment please."
"Gozi speaking,"
"Hi."
"How are you?"
"Not on this number– I'm in New York."
"Oh, the conference."
"Yeah."
"The PA called right?"
"Yes." George answered.
"She stepped out; I'll grab your chart."
"Is that for me?" George could hear the physician's assistant in the background.

"It is," Gozi said in the distance.

George sat on hold for twenty seconds that had all the trappings of thirty minutes. *She was right there; what is taking her so long to pick up the phone?* he thought.

"Betty here. George, I have your charts.

"Your test came back ok but there are a few concerns the doctor has, nothing to rush home about but when you return, Dr. Angelo would like to go over everything with you."

"Sounds like a plan," George answered. But everything seems good?"

"Yes. X-rays show just what Dr. Angelo expected. The tumor is shrinking and the treatments seem to be working in your favor."

"That's excellent news!" George answered. "I was getting prepared to head back home on the next flight.

"No, you're good." Betty reassured him. George hung up and called home.

"Baby, I just spoke with the doctor's office and everything seems to be fine. She has a few concerns she wants to speak with me about when I return, but nothing to worry about."

CHAPTER THREE: THE CONFERENCE

"Oh, that's good news, honey, I was wondering why they called twice in one day."

"Oh, she said the first call was a mistake. Gotta check into the hotel, kids ok?"

"Yes, Jason's at soccer and will ride home with Jimmy's mom."

"Love you - bye."

***

George picked up his thick, tattered notebook. In it he carried notes on investing, especially in gold and silver. This conference was to be a dream come true; a place where ideas from the investor would be heard, where the 'experts' had no greater say than the lay people; a place where precious metals were given their proper treatment. He approached the hotel desk.

"Reservation number 53189."

"Yes, we have it here, nice to see you back. One or two keys?"

"Two please, always need a backup plan," George told the desk clerk.

"Sir - are you ok?" The clerk asked in a heavy Spanish accent.

George was gripping the right side of his lower chest, his face squinting more from confusion than from pain.

"I'm ok." George said.

"I'm just...let me sit down for a moment."

George unwrapped the half turkey sandwich in his satchel – he always had one without mayonnaise packed for each trip, and took a couple of bites.

"I just need to eat."

The clerk moved from behind the desk and pulled up a chair.

"Front desk to manager." She radioed out.

"No – no. I'm fine; it's just little discomfort. Had some tests done before traveling and was bruised a little."

"Do you need a doctor?" The clerk asked.

"Oh no; I'm going to my room to lay down for a bit before the conference."

"Ok – well, let us know if there's anything we can do."

George sat there for another few minutes and headed toward the elevators. Over the last three years, he ignored pain and discomfort until going to the doctor six months earlier. They found a mass in his chest and treated it aggressively with chemo. It worked, but the results of the treatments were nearly as painful as the mass itself. George was constantly grabbing his chest in an effort to squeeze the pain away. He was in New York for the week-long, one of a kind investors' conference called, "The Combine," and didn't want anything to stand in the way of full participation.

Conference speakers would be discussing all asset classes: stocks, bonds, commodities, especially gold and silver, but all from a fresh perspective. Each asset class was presented much like assessing athletes trying out for an NFL team. One asset class was categorized as defense, the others - offense. The speakers were not just money managers or financial analysts. Coaches from sports and business were also offering advice on how a winning team is put together. Everyone has to play their part. If a 'player' or investment was to make the portfolio team, the investment had to exhibit the same qualities of a great human player . . .resilience, balance and strength.

CHAPTER THREE: THE CONFERENCE

***

The alarm clock rang at 7:15 pm; George didn't answer. The conference started at 8:00 pm but was only a mile away. His wife, Carol, called his cell phone to check on him - no answer.

At 7:45, three hard knocks on the door. "Bang! Bang! Bang!"

Three more knocks, and then a call from the hotel hallway.

"George, you in there?" Craig, his childhood friend from Jersey, was to meet him in the lobby at 7:30.

Craig began feeling uncomfortable. Then a voice.

"I'm up." George ran to the door and opened it.

"Must have overslept."

"Dude – it's almost 8;we gotta go!"

George hurriedly got dressed.

That's weird, George thought. *I never oversleep.* He grabbed his briefcase, and headed out.

"Sorry about that man - don't know what happened." Craig shrugged as they made their way to the elevators.

"It happens."

This conference was entirely too important. Outside, they sprinted toward the car.

"It's this way!" Craig called out, pointing ahead. George tried to keep up, but his legs felt like cement pillars not meant to move. His chest constricted. He struggled to keep up, but the distance between them was lengthening with each stride.

"I'm coming!" George shouted. He was out of breath, and slowed to a walk. Although 215 pounds and 6'3, George kept himself in good shape.

I'm going to have to start working out more, he thought. "Now that I'm able to. Lung cancer can't hold me back anymore. We beat it!" he whispered to himself.

Craig was waiting in the car when George climbed in. "We got five minutes." Craig said. "Let's do this!"

***

Once in the conference hall, George sat down at the far end of an oval table next to business people from around the globe. The idea behind this financial *combine* was borrowed from professional sports where NFL teams come together to research which players they should draft. The idea had resonated. Everyone wanted to put together their *investment team*. Investors liked the idea of putting asset classes through a rudimentary exercise where they could eliminate the weak and keep the strong.

George set his briefcase on the floor and straightened his tie. Reaching for his water, he took a moment to calm his mind, but he wasn't feeling his best. The music started; it was the NFL theme song and the audience cheered like they were in a sports arena. Anticipation filled the air as the curtain rose and lights illuminated the stage.

***

Enter Thomas Harkins - the mastermind behind the combine conference. Harkins was a unique guy. He wore Chicago Oxford bespoke, a strong jaw line, and sleek black hair. He was humbly confident, an odd hybrid. He stepped to the microphone.

"Welcome to the first annual investment combine!" The crowd orupted in applause.

CHAPTER THREE: THE CONFERENCE

"Thank you for joining us today. Have you ever once stopped to question why investment portfolios are designed the way they are? Depending on your age, your investments may be heavily weighted in stocks or a hybrid of stocks and bonds. No questions asked because the premise has been firmly established. Most investors assume an exclusive mixture of stocks and bonds is the right approach, the prudent approach; after all, millions of people can't be wrong - until they are. Prepare to be changed."

The crowd interrupted Harkins with random whistles of affirmation. He continued.

"We are thrilled you took the time from your busy schedules to come make history. Today will change the face of financial services – forever," Harkins said - his voice filling the room with its deep and rich Midwestern tones.

George looked around the room. It was packed wall to wall with people. So many had lost over the past few years; so many wanted to take control of their financial lives. So many were tired of being told what to do with their money only to find that their advisors knew little more than they did about what worked.

From the front, Harkins spoke, "Anything that works in life has a structure, has a lead, and has a supporting cast. We designed the combine approach because traditional investment theories don't work anymore. This is difficult for most to accept as it relates to their money, although they readily accept it in every other area of their lives. The pay phone, the eight track tape and the Sony Walkman were great innovations when introduced. Companies made billions but what happened? The market continued to evolve. Imagine me standing here trying to convince you how the new Walkman is going to replace the iPod. Why would you laugh? You would laugh because evolution doesn't revert. Evolution always moves forward or it dies – no in-between. Today, Wall Street is the Sony Walkman. Knowledge and innovation has passed it by, but they continue to tell us that they're still relevant. They are not. When you place your money in the hands of investment firms who have no negative consequence if you fail, but favorable consequence when you succeed, you aren't moving forward – it is backward evolution which by definition is deterioration. "Many of you here are business owners. You live and die on your decisions – and you can live with that. Most of us don't want to live and die on the decisions of another. Today, we intend to provide you with the data so you can start making decisions for you. What a novel idea. Today, you start investing in yourself."

George was listening but distracted. He reached for his water again. His breathing was short. He began pulling on his chest.

Why am I so tired? George thought. Seemed the couple hours of sleep had done more harm than good. *Maybe I...*

"Whatcha think, man?" Craig interrupted his thoughts.

"This is great stuff!" George replied and gave a thumbs up.

Thomas Harkins introduced the first speaker. "First, we will have David Monk explain the overview of our approach and more details on what we plan to accomplish here this weekend. Monk will share our vision."

George tried to center his thoughts. He took out his pen and unfolded the handout entitled, "The Golden Rule." From the corner of his eye, he could feel Craig looking at him with concern.

"Without further ado," Harkins said, "David Monk!"

The audience stood to their feet in a reception more indicative of respect than artificial fanfare. Monk is a mental

CHAPTER THREE: THE CONFERENCE

machine. His ideas on the capital markets, gold and silver have found international acceptance for one reason alone – he highlights common sense. He has found common sense to be rare as gold itself. Monk is famous for rejecting false premise, especially false premise that affects what wealthy people do with their money. He's become somewhat of a specialist in the area of re-evaluating financial assertions that foster ill-advised peripheral decisions.

A unique creature in every sense, he walks with a confidence school can't give. He carries tattoos on his arms, forearms, wrists and neck. If one isn't careful, it's easy to judge the man before hearing him speak, but all who hold judgment profit handsomely from rejecting stereotype. His very existence is a lesson in false premise. He's everything Wall Street wishes it had, authenticity.

Stepping to the microphone, Monk spoke, "False premise is a spider – a poisonous spider at that. The tentacles of false premise dig deep into the hearts and minds of every human being. Premise trumps reality because reality must first past through premise before we process it. Reality must argue against premise before we will accept it, if ever. If you woke up in Miami in May and your windows were frozen, with heavy flakes of snow falling in the spring, your premise that this cannot and does not happen in Miami would argue against the fact that it was indeed happening right in front of your eyes. This is because the weight of history is heavy and can barely be lifted by the mind resistant to seeing things differently. The good news is that fresh perspective is also heavy. And it is able to adequately confront the old mindset and avoid being trapped by the perspective of the past. The past isn't bad, it's just over."

Small claps rolled into larger ones. Monk paused and continued, "Thinking differently doesn't just happen by default. It is a proactive phenomenon. You must make innovative assumptions against how things have always been to even remotely have a chance of changing the way things are now. Let's press in closer on the power of premise. I have a question." Monk continued, "What does a pilot look like, a doctor, a scientist, a musician? Without trying, each person has instantly imagined what people in these particular professions look like or 'should' look like. This is good and bad. Good because everything must have a baseline if for nothing else, to establish a foundation. But money isn't a uniform profession; money is an intellectual sport. The stereotypical advisor with the stereotypical education has failed the stereotypical wealthy investor. Few talk about what I'm about to say.

As a society, we aren't settled with people who step outside the lines and become successful, especially if these people operate with prudence, thoughtfulness and discipline, attributions associated with the educated mind. In essence, unlicensed intellect bothers most people. We don't mind the rogue who lives on a mountain and does whatever mountain people do, but we get jumpy when someone steps into our world, flips our assumptions upside down, and is successful doing so. A Florida Highway patrolman told me a story years ago that I'll never forget.

***

Traveling north on Interstate Highway 75 in south Florida, a woman he only called Loretta came upon a horrible crash. An elderly couple riding on a motorcycle and attached sidecar had swerved to avoid highway debris and tipped over at 70MPH. Traffic was just coming to a standstill as Loretta slowed to learn the cause of the sudden stop.

CHAPTER THREE: THE CONFERENCE

She pulled over, got out of the car and ran to the couple.

The man was on the shoulder of the road, bleeding profusely from under his helmet. The woman had been thrown into the median with what seemed to be fatal wounds to the midsection of her body. As other drivers ran up behind Loretta, she put the strangers to work.

She instructed one man to hold the driver's head straight and another to hold one side of his helmet as Loretta slipped her hand underneath the mouth portion. The driver was drowning in his own blood and needed an airway now.

"Slowly," Loretta instructed another passerby.

"One, two, three – lift." The three removed the man's helmet and got an airway established.

"Stay here and hold this in his mouth." Loretta instructed handing the passerby a wooden stick to keep the man from swallowing his tongue.

She then ran to the median where the woman was groaning in what sounded like the last sounds she would make. Two men walked up.

"We're doctors," both men said.

"Good," Loretta responded.

She proceeded to give an accurate medical assessment, detailing where she thought the most severed injuries were, and what needed to be done to save both patients. Other drivers had called 911 and Loretta figured her job and the job of the newly arrived physicians was to keep the couple alive for the next fifteen minutes until the helicopter could land and get the injured to a hospital.

The helicopter landed in the middle of the highway. She had succeeded. The gentleman and his wife had been stabilized for transport. Walking back to her car next to the two physicians she looked down to see her clothes soaked in blood. One particularly impressed physician asked her a question as their paths parted respectively towards their cars.

"So where do you practice?" the physician asked.

Loretta stopped walking, turned and looked the physician in the eye with a smile. "I'm not a doctor," she said.

"Surely you are," the physician responded. "Your level of medical knowledge was evident."

"Thank you, but I never got accepted into medical school; they said I didn't have what it took, so I just read the books on my own." Loretta said.

The doctor stepped back and removed his cap to better grip his forehead.

"Are you kidding me?" the doctor asked.

"I wish I was."

What do you do when a person can just do the job? What do you do when reality forces you to skip past the 'what qualifies you to do this' stage and into the 'I just saw you do it' stage? And that's the complexity of premise. The doctors walked up, giving their credentials; Loretta showed her credentials by saving lives. Which one would you want working on you in the middle of that highway?"

***

The audience was now on the edge of their seats. Monk removed the microphone from its stand and with rounded shoulders under a purple shirt, continued speaking. "Friends, common sense is routinely ignored, so much so that when you give simple answers to complex problems, people think it's a trick. Nowhere is this more problematic than in the financial services industry. The Wall Street model is based on gathering 'qualified' individuals to promote investment opportunities to the uninformed investing public. What the public buys

CHAPTER THREE: THE CONFERENCE

provides liquidity for these same Wall Street individuals to sell. The game is rigged. When you look at what's in front of us, one fact stands above the rest. Wall Street is a cash cow producing very expensive milk. This cannot be overstated. If the average Joe happens to make money from investing in Wall Street, it is an indirect consequence of first benefitting someone else. In other words, profits given to the average Joe are the bread crumbs Wall Street forgot to clean up behind them. Hear me clearly; Wall Street's agenda isn't to make you rich. It is to keep them rich. The only person who has *you* as a priority – is you."

The room was pin drop silent. Monk continued., "So how does one play such a rigged game? You play with the most effective tool used in any such game – information. If I told you there was a meteor headed for your house that will land in 30 minutes, what would you do? The beautiful thing about my warning is that you have time to adjust, gather personal belongings, family and maybe a few friends before you leave your house. You may even have time to feed the cat. The odd thing is this; you can warn some people about the meteor and they will think they have longer than 30 minutes. These kinds of people will assume they actually have 45 minutes. It isn't that this type of person doesn't believe you. No, it's much worse; they do believe you but they believe your timing is off. And the only thing worse than suffering from a bad event is in the middle of the suffering realizing that you actually had time to save yourself."

George felt invigorated by these words. This is exactly what he came to hear. Frank information. He'd held the same philosophy for years, but trying to communicate it to others, especially financial advisors, always frustrated him.

Monk picked up his notebook, organized his papers and left the podium with these last comments, "As you put together your investment 'teams' today, expect to feel weird. This is because you aren't supposed to know what you're doing. The experts are supposed to know. You aren't supposed to be qualified to make decisions about your finances – we've been taught that somebody else should do that for us. They should not. Saving yourself is a foreign concept to the investing public. Lesson number one is this: no one's going save you. What you don't do for you will not be done. If you sit around and invest your retirement accounts in corporations you believe are well-managed, you may be surprised to learn months before your scheduled retirement how mismanaged these companies were. If you lose your savings because of a market crash, no one is going to return a dollar to you. No one is going to pay you for all your years of commitment as a faithful stockholder. You are the owner of your team; you are the coach and today you pick your players. It's your life, manage it to win."

The room exploded with applause. George had written copious notes. As a business owner, this was the answer he was seeking. Better said, this was the conformation of the answer he already knew. Take control of your money using proper information, especially information you're frequently encouraged to stay away from.

"Shrimp?" the waiter asked.

"No, I'm good. I will have another water." George said.

George, 62, at one point, had over $5 million in his portfolio, today, less than $2.5 million. Other business owners at the table had their own stories of loss and dissatisfaction with the traditional investment advice they had received

CHAPTER THREE: THE CONFERENCE

over the years. There was a new energy, a new impetus for independent thinking in the air. You could feel it.

"I've invested in stocks and bonds my entire life," one attendee at his table commented. "I've always wanted to have exposure to silver, gold and other commodities. It's time," he said. "It's time."

"I agree wholeheartedly," George responded.

"The worse that can happen is what is happening now," another silver-haired man at the table contributed to the conversation. "Stocks and bonds aren't bad, they aren't wrong, they are just incomplete. I want to use all available options and give myself the best chance. I want to give my portfolio, my investment 'team' the best chance to win."

"Excuse me, gentlemen," George got up to use the restroom. Standing over the urinal, George clutched his chest. He looked back towards the door. The handle was moving although it was still.

What's going on with me? he wondered. While repeatedly licking his lips, he began sweating heavily. Sounds from the conference were piped into the restroom and he could hear the next speaker beginning his presentation.

"Now if everyone will look at page nine from the handout we distributed earlier…" George washed his hands and headed back out the door as another attendee was headed in. "Great conference, huh?" the man said.

George didn't answer.

Craig saw him walking back to their table. He didn't look like himself.

"You ok, man?"

"Not really," George answered under his breath.

"Head back to the hotel and I'll bring everything from the meeting to you later on," Craig suggested.

The speaker continued.

"If we... if we look at the margin on the right of the page, we can see that..."

"Did he say page nine?" George asked.

"Yes, right here," Craig looked over and saw George was looking at his book upside down.

"Let's compare the S & P, The Russell and the DOW against silver and gold."

George closed his eyes while listening; the darkness made him feel better.

"This chart details the uncorrelated nature of..."

A woman screamed.

Audience members jumped to their feet, each looking around for the source of the voice. Confusion quickly populated the room.

Craig looked behind him only to see the cause of the scream was in front of him. George had passed out and was laying on the floor in full seizure.

"Oh God! Call 911!" Craig yelled.

Screeching feedback from the microphone echoed the room as Monk looked around those blocking his view.

"Ladies and gentlemen, we have some type of disturbance, please bear with us," he said.

"We need a doctor!" one attendee shouted across the room.

A tall, thin man in a blue blazer and white linen shirt pushed through the small mob.

"Excuse me - excuse me, I'm a doctor!"

Craig ushered him to his friend.

"Let's take a thirty minute break as the authorities attend to an emergency," the speaker announced.

"Sir, what is your name?" the doctor asked peering down at the body on the floor.

CHAPTER THREE: THE CONFERENCE

George didn't answer.

"His name is George," Craig inserted. The doctor was taking his pulse and turning George over onto his back.

"Paramedics are on the way," Craig told the doctor.

"Do you know anything about his medical history?" the doctor asked Craig while checking George's wrists and neck for any medical tags.

"He had lung cancer, but recently got news it was gone and he was doing well."

"How do you know that," the doctor asked. "Based on what premise?"

Craig was a bit taken by the skeptical tone of the question; he didn't really know how to answer.

"Well, he told me he was doing better.

The doctor didn't respond.

"Make a path!" The doctor yelled to the groups of people standing around. "We have to get him out of here."

The paramedics made their way through the crowed. The doctor was supporting George's head with his hands.

"You're going to be fine, sir; we just need to get you to the hospital."

"Take him to Beth Israel; I'm on staff." The doctor told the paramedics.

***

Craig paced the emergency room as the doctors connected George to multiple monitoring systems. He tried to get George's wife on the phone but only got voicemail.

"Carol, this is Craig from Jersey. Need you to call me right away."

"Sir, the hospital needs some identifying information on your friend," the hospital insurance representative asked Craig.

"What is the patient's name?" she asked.
"His name is George."
"Last name?"
"Stanley."

Chapter Four
THE TRANSCRIPT

CHAPTER FOUR: THE TRANSCRIPT

BY THE TIME GEORGE FELT WELL ENOUGH to return to his hotel, the sun was flirting with rising. His friend, Craig, would go back to the conference information desk and pick up transcripts from the class they missed, David Monk's class on gold. George was oscillating between feeling stronger and weaker, depending on the time of day. Originally, he was going back to Austin early, but reconsidered, and he made Craig promise not to tell Carol the extent of what really happened. In George's mind, the doctors had released him. Surely, if it had been serious, the doctors wouldn't have allowed him to leave the hospital. Furthermore, prior to leaving Austin, Dr. Angelo had confirmed he was better, the biopsy was good news, tumors were nearly gone, and he was in remission. But something still didn't feel right. George wanted to believe he was better – but this episode away from home would suggest there still may be a problem. Maybe it was only in his mind.

Back in his room, George moved the food tray off his bed, sat up, and grabbed the transcript Craig dropped off. The heading read:

Anything of value, in low circulation, will always increase in value.

Looks like David Monk had continued right where he left off. George thought to himself, beginning to read Monk's comments.

> "Raise your hand if you're greedy. (laughter) Wall Street has trained you to think that everything you do is out of greed, that you're a greedy monster," the notes read. "I have to admit, it's a brilliant strategy. It's brilliant because Wall Street first gently condemns your desire for excess money - and then provides a path to get it. It would be like your local Weight Watchers office selling the most fattening cheesecake at their checkout counter. It's brilliant because you wouldn't have a need

57

for them unless you were overweight so they guarantee their existence by keeping you fat . . . diabolical - but profitable. That said, this next statement may surprise you - I like Wall Street. I like it because I understand it. Because I am clear on its purpose. And when you're clear on its purpose, you can use it for your purpose. The truth is this, you, like most Americans, invest not because you want so much more, but because you're concerned about losing what you have. Most people invest for the same reason you buy a security system for your home. Everything you love, everything you own is inside; the system doesn't make your house bigger, it only protects what's already inside. And for most of us, that is the essence of why we invest at this point in our lives. Our investments are a security system.

Don't get me wrong - everybody likes making money, and a lot of it, but wealth preservation is the new profit. You can make money by not losing any. Things have changed. In this economy, if I can show you a performance that maintains even value instead of losing money, and helps you to build equity, you're going to be more satisfied than not."

George looked up, considering what he'd just read. That was true, and went along with what he'd been thinking for years. His portfolio was down fifty percent from where it had been several years earlier, and he was feeling desperate. Not desperate to make more money, but desperate to get back the money he'd already made. He wanted to protect more than to gain. Monk's words resonated with him. He looked down, and continued to read.

"Not even greedy people want to be told they're

CHAPTER FOUR: THE TRANSCRIPT

greedy. Even people who are greedy dislike it when there's someone on the phone saying, 'There's a way to get rich on this thing.' We don't mind getting rich, but we just don't want it phrased that way. That's because people want to be told how to manage an economic storm. No one plans for sunshine; people plan for storms. Now each person determines what the term 'manage' means to them. For one guy, managing an economic storm means maintaining $10 million a year; for another, this term means maintaining $10 million in value against inflation; same amounts but one person wants to maintain while the other wants to gain. Money is always relative. I remember a time in this country when you worked, retired, got your pension, and moved to Florida. Not because you wanted to, but because it was expected. That's what everyone did. If you lived on the East Coast, Florida was the place. On the West Coast, maybe you moved down to San Diego, away from the rush of LA or San Francisco. You'd buy your house with cash and live the rest of your life playing golf. And that's just the way it was.

But look at the people who are retired *now*. Not so much the Baby Boomer generation, but the generation before that. I can still remember my grandfather owning a construction business in New York. He wasn't rich, but he certainly had enough money to keep him and my grandmother comfortable and safe. But in his older age, I had to buy a car for him because he couldn't afford one himself. Between the stock market and bad investments, things got so bad my grandparents were looking at doing a reverse mortgage, just to get by."

Monk explained.

George paused again, adjusted his reading glasses and looked up. Monk was right; this was exactly what happened to him. The economy had gone downhill quickly, and with it, the stock market. Now people were beginning to accept that everyone lost money. That losing was normal. And Wall Street was fostering that belief, while preparing to promote a new story of how everyone can get their money back – through Wall Street, of course.

Wall Street had become the Weight Watchers office selling fattening cheesecake at the checkout counter. All of this was making sense in a way that began to upset George. Upsetting because it was so obvious, so obvious you couldn't see it. He kept reading.

"The investors of America need to stand up and learn a new philosophy: one of active optimism and action. They need to replace the old Wall Street philosophy with a new one, one that places the concentration on maintaining your lifestyle, not the lifestyle of the bankers. The place to start with this new approach is precious metals investing. Investing in precious metals is an anomaly to traditional Wall Street speak. How many times have you watched financial television and heard one of the hosts say 'You should invest in gold or silver?' Rarely if ever. But you've heard countless times how speculative such investments are, although you've never fully understood the logic behind why they call precious metals 'speculative' – and you haven't understood the logic because there is none. Let's just think about what we're saying for a moment. Is there anything in your life that you consider precious that is

CHAPTER FOUR: THE TRANSCRIPT

speculative? Anything? Any person? In fact, it is just the opposite. If you went out and purchased a precious, rare Leonardo de Vinci painting, a rare diamond, or a 1968 Mustang, would there be anything speculative about these purchases? Nope. The reason is, such purchases highlight the most fundamental principle of capitalism. *Anything of value, in low circulation, will always increase in value.* The very idea of speculative investing is based on a person not knowing whether something will increase in value. This fits perfectly in the area of common stock and the like, but is an inappropriate description of precious metals. Before one makes strides into understanding precious metals, you have to first disassemble the false narrative that has kept you way from them all these years.

Precious metals place you in a position of leadership, strength, and global financial security. When you own gold and silver, you aren't looking for a market, you are a market."

Monk continued.

"In other words, you – the investor in precious metals – becomes the holder of value, instead of seeking value, instead of following the story given to you and mindlessly following the script. But not only that, the precious metals discussion fits into an alternative view, a constitutional view. It gives you choice, which you didn't really have before. People are beginning to understand that even independent research houses on Wall Street aren't independent, that everyone is in bed with everyone else, a financial orgy. Again, I like Wall

Street, because I understand it."

Wow, George thought to himself.

"Of course, the mainstream media – and the uninformed public – all work hard to tell you that it's possible to get rich quick, which makes you feel greedy, which makes you feel guilty and the circle just goes round and round. The media will feature the $250 million lotto winner, or the stock that did 800 percent in three months. And then investors get burned badly, trying to accomplish what they've seen other people do. The truth is, there's no get-rich-quick scheme, on Wall Street or anywhere else. In the end, it's a matter of being smart, staying safe, and investing in stability. The most stable way to keep up with the pace of inflation and really prosper when this economy takes the next drastic turn is investing in physical gold and silver. But again, the Wall Street narrative is powerful. Never underestimate its influence on your thought processes.

To highlight the narrative power of Wall Street and how this power can have profound implications on the investment community, consider this. If the *Wall Street Journal* ran a front page headline that said,

'Buy gold now before it's too late!'

Gold would become a bubble. Gold would skyrocket to $6000; everyone would jump on board. The last people in would get their asses handed to them in a woven basket, and the gold would fall back. That is

CHAPTER FOUR: THE TRANSCRIPT

the power of story. That's the power of premise. It is very important to understand one thing; when an individual authority or an authoritative institution says something is so, it becomes so, even if only temporarily. Authorities can suspend reality long enough that you're pulled into a fantasy. By the time reality kicks in, it's too late."

George sat back and frowned. He'd been with David up to this point, but Monk seemed to be contradicting himself a bit now. Gold gave investors a chance to partner with security, to be active with their investments. Now he seemed to be saying that it wouldn't work in the long term if everyone bought it. But gold was real money so it shouldn't matter if the general public started buying it, should it? The general public has been purchasing stocks for hundreds of years, and stocks are still around, being sold everyday. What did Monk mean? He kept reading.

"I know what you're thinking right now – that I'm contradicting myself." (George smiled.) "The thing about gold, though, is that gold and silver have fundamental value. They have fundamental reasons to increase in price. That doesn't mean that the media won't push that market faster or slow it down, but fundamentally, nothing changes. If silver pulled back from $34 to $30, I'm not going to say, 'Oh my God, let me get out of silver,' because fundamentally, silver still has to go up in the end. If gold pulls back to $1600, I'm buying more. I will buy every ounce I can get my hands on because, fundamentally, nothing changes and the gold is still worth its weight in, well, gold. And until the fundamentals of this economy and the global economy change, nothing is going to change the gold market. Until currency stabilizes, gold is the only sure bet."

So how do we stabilize currency? George asked himself, the question he would have asked in the class.

He tugged on his chest, gazed out the open window in his hotel room, then bent over the notes again to see if Monk had answered that question.

"So if gold is the only stable bet, how does the United States of America take advantage of that? The answer is simple: the US has to start buying gold again, and stop selling it. Government is as dependent on gold as the individual investor is, and yet they're selling it instead of buying it. Why? China has been buying every ounce of gold they can get their hands on for the past thirty years, but their currency isn't pegged to gold. It doesn't matter to them if the price of gold goes up or down. That's why they buy it by the metric ton at $1700 an ounce. They're not looking at the short-term. Ever since August 15, 1971 when Nixon took the US off the gold standard entirely, we've been selling as much gold as we can just to keep the price down. Remember, anything of value, in low circulation, always increases in value. But the opposite is true, anything of value that increases in circulation, lowers in value. But remember, gold can only be discovered, never made. There is a finite amount of gold in existence. Gold cannot be synthetically produced like the paper money in your pocket. There are no gold printing presses, which is one of the reasons gold will never be worth zero or become a hyperinflationary

CHAPTER FOUR: THE TRANSCRIPT

financial product. Think about that.

Based upon what we know the US had in Fort Knox in the early '70s, compared to what the government has told us they've put on the exchange in London, we've inflated our dollar beyond repair. That's because our dollar *is* dependent on the price of gold. This is what destabilizes the dollar, but that brings me back to what we know – that gold is the surest bet on the planet."

Suddenly George's lungs constricted and he gasped. *Talk about taking care of yourself,* he thought. None of this information was going to do him any good if he didn't live to use it. He waited a moment, reached for a glass of water, and in doing so, spilled it over the transcript.
"Shit."
He wiped away most of what he could, smearing some of the words in the process - took another deep breath and a drink of the little water left. It made him feel a bit better, though he still wanted to lie down and go to sleep. He was scheduled for a flight the next day, and had already called his doctor to let her know that her office was going to be his first stop.

The doctors at the hospital had been less than helpful, telling him only that he needed to get back to his doctor soon, but then they let him go back to the hotel, which confused him. Dr. Angelo had told him his cancer was in remission. But something wasn't right.

George wanted desperately to stay at the conference. The speakers were giving him the information he craved, and even encouraging him to ask questions, letting him know that it was okay to wonder about the traditional approach to

65

investing and make his own judgments. It was exactly what he needed in his investing life. But if he couldn't go back to the conference itself, perhaps he should just go home. Maybe it was time to go home. He'd visit Dr. Angelo as soon as he returned. George had called Gozi to get her opinion and she seemed to think he should be fine, and so he stayed in New York one extra day.

David Monk's advice was going to be very important in the coming months, as he reordered his portfolio. With that thought, he turned back to the transcription in front of him.

"The thing is this: there are a lot of people who don't want to hear about investing in gold. They don't want to think about it. Wall Street has spent years and years telling them that the stock market is the only choice, and down playing the idea of investing in gold. We see it every day in my company. You'd be surprised how many people hang up because deep down, they know that gold is the only safe investment, but in order to accept that, you have to accept the fact that the system is rigged and that maybe you've been wrong all these years.

What the financial advisors are trying to hide from their clients, though, is that everyone is right back where they were four or five years ago – they haven't made any money, and they've slipped backwards because of time decay. You will never hear an advisor tell you, 'Well, you've gained all your losses back but you've lost five years of life while waiting.' That doesn't feel like progress, does it?

People have to learn to look at their money in a

CHAPTER FOUR: THE TRANSCRIPT

different way. Instead of saying, 'Well, I'm not losing as much as my neighbor is,' they should be saying, 'How can I *make* money at this time?' or 'how can I preserve the money I've already made?' Look at the Great Depression, the Rockefellers, the Rothschilds, and the Morgans. These families acquired wealth that broke the boundary of generations, when other people were losing everything. So yes, for many, the Great Depression was horrible, but not for the Warburgs. They certainly weren't sitting there saying, *'Oh, what a horrible tragedy this is, but at least I'm not losing as much as that guy over there.'* They found a way to maintain and profit. And that's exactly where we are today.

That's why I'm here. That's why I'm giving you the information you need to protect yourself and stop your portfolio from bleeding to death. The information you need to start acting for yourself, instead of following a script that was written for you – without your input."

George turned to the last page of the transcript.

"So why should the investing public invest in gold, and why now? It's not really a matter of doing it now. It's the fact that it should have been done years ago. Now we're getting to the point where if it's not done soon, it's going to be too late. The system has been broken for a long time, and people should have been protecting themselves, and told there were alternative ways and strategies to do so, but they were not. There's no more time to waste.

So on to an obvious question – if you *do* buy gold,

where do you store it? Who wants to have gold in their garage, or in some storage house in Minnesota? From a practical standpoint, is it possible for people to actually have physical gold and take delivery of it?

I'm here to tell you that there is a way to make it practical. A portion of physical gold and silver sitting in a safe is something that I encourage everybody to do, to some extent. But as far as an overall savings and liquidity - there are options. There are opportunities to have accounts through the Delaware Depository, through multinational clearance firms. This gives you liquidity that equals a standard bank account. This can be something that's looked at as a savings vehicle, as much as it is an investment vehicle. Those firms hold gold for you, and give you a payout if you need it. Unless we see some drastic changes in this country, which I don't see happening as far as our overall monetary policy, then what we've seen over the past ten years is the tip of the iceberg compared to what we're going to see in the next ten years. The good thing is, just because everyone else is suffering doesn't mean you have to."

END OF TRANSCRIPT

CHAPTER FOUR: THE TRANSCRIPT

George leaned back and let the papers fall to the table in front of him; he realized that he'd been holding his breath. This was what he'd been searching for – someone to tell him the truth, and encourage him to make his own decisions. Now it looked like, by hook or by crook, he'd found that person.

Despite the pain in his chest, he couldn't go home now; he had to get back to the conference. To hear what other people were saying, talk to them about possibilities. Each table was a brainstorming session – men and women throwing ideas out there, discussing them, and then moving on to new options.

Most of all, though, he had questions and he wanted answers. He wanted to hear what other people at the conference thought, and he wanted to take his questions to the professionals. If he could, he would get some of the presenters into private conversations and ask for personal advice and viewpoints. He had to get back into that conference, regardless of the tight feeling in his chest.

Chapter Five
THE CODE

CHAPTER FIVE: THE CODE

THE ROOM WAS EERILY SILENT, but for the gritty sound of stubble being caressed by worried fingers. Stan was still there – still sitting at his desk in Austin, Texas. His shirt was now soaked, his knuckles snow white, and his nerves shot. Killing yourself is nerve racking. He'd been interrupted right when he was going to pull the trigger. Was it a sign from God? Something he should listen to or random coincidence?

Regardless, the interruption had given him time to think, and that was enough to kill his willpower. He was second guessing the decision he thought he'd already made – the decision to end his life.

The slight pause had given him time to think about all the questions too obvious to consider in the midst of depression. What about his family? There would be life insurance, of course, but not nearly enough. Further, the insurance wouldn't be redeemable if his death was deemed a suicide, but that's what depression does. It clouds judgment by taking the worse possible option and hiding its consequences. His little Jesse would have to grow up without him. Wasn't she going to have to do that already? Why expedite the process? Stan's thoughts ran wild. And why was the doctor calling anyway? He didn't need any more bad news so he decided he'd call back in the morning. The initial news from the doctor had already been enough to tip him over the edge.

The phone that saved him began vibrating again; he snapped out of the fog and hurriedly turned the phone right side up. He went to answer, but before he could, it stopped. His hand moved instead to the picture of Jesse, still face-down on the desk. He propped it up again, smiling tenderly at the girl – the light of his life. The glass frame caught a ray of light and became a mirror, so that Stan's own face overshadowed his daughter's. What he saw shocked him. His eyes were glassy and full of exhaustion, his complexion gray and sagging. He

THE PREMISE, THE MONEY & THE GOLD

looked about seventy years old. Like a man who had given up; the look that crawls onto the face after dreams in the heart have been brutally crushed.

What am I doing? he thought. Ten seconds of a phone ringing had given his conscious mind a chance to kick into gear again. Gone was the faded, quiet mindlessness of his depression. In its place, he found a cold, clear resolve. He'd been a fool to think that killing himself was the answer. There were other answers; there always are.

Until now, his life had been planned down to the minute, but dying early was a variable he never considered. In an odd way, taking his life would put his life back in his own hands. He would control the time and place – he would engineer the end. But he backed away from the precipice. Jesse loved him too much.

"Oh, God help me," he mumbled.

Stan wasn't a religious man, but all find religion when faced with an uncertain eternity, even if only a pragmatic function. Better to believe in God and be wrong than not to believe and be wrong. In this moment of intense despair, Stan slid out of his chair and onto the floor.

"Hello?" Stan said looking at the ceiling. "If you can hear me – please help." Stan prayed for the first time in his life – his eyes wide open.

"I don't know if I'm a good enough person to pray, sir, and I've never been to church, but I did read one time that you help those who are weak. I read that you will help people who don't have anybody to turn to. I read where you have mercy on them, even those who aren't Christians. Sir, I am not a Christian; I'm an engineer – but I'm asking for you to help me. I don't know if the prayer will get through the ceiling or if I'll make it through another day, but thank you for listening and I'll appreciate any assistance."

CHAPTER FIVE: THE CODE

Stan's' shirt was polka-dotted with tears as he moved from his knees and sat on the back of his legs.

"Well – Thank you again for listening."

Stan grunted and got up. He began to hear the sounds of faint happiness. Jesse was playing upstairs and the butterfly noise began easing through the walls. She was singing, "If that mockingbird don't sing, mama's gonna buy you a diamond ring."

My Jesse, he thought, smiling broadly. Just then, the door opened.

"Daddy?" Jesse's voice echoed from atop the stairs. She was headed his way.

Stan quickly dialed in the code to his top drawer, anxious to put the gun back in its place before his daughter saw it. But his hands slipped, and he hit one wrong number. He yanked on the drawer but it wouldn't open. Feverishly, he began punching numbers again.

"Yes, dear?" he yelled back.

Jesse's footsteps began their seven-second trip down the stairs, led by the sound of her voice. "If that diamond ring don't shine…"

Stan's hands were moist with sweat. He gripped the knob of the drawer and tried once more.

"One! Nine! Thirty-Seven!" he repeated the code under his breath.

The drawer popped open.

Stan pushed the gun back in and slammed it shut just as Jesse rounded the corner. She stood perfectly still.

"Daddy, whatcha' doing?"

Stan paused, trying to think of an appropriate answer. He thought about lying, but reconsidered. She deserved better than that. He let out a deep breath.

"Dad's just thinking, baby."

"Thinking 'bout what?"

"About how much I love you and how proud I am of you."

She smiled, ran into his arms, and gave him a big kiss on the cheek. "Daddy, I want to be just like you when I grow up," she said.

"But you're a little girl."

"I still want to be like you."

As they embraced, his smile deteriorated as he rested his chin on her tiny shoulder. He knew what almost happened. Stan had a clear thought. *I have little time left. I have to get things together for this little one. I have to secure her future and that of Nicole's, I can't give up now.*

***

Three days later, Stan sat in his advisor's office filling out A-CAT forms to transfer his $800,000 account to a competing firm, one that allowed for precious metals investing. In his mind, if he was going to leave his money behind, he wanted it in a form that would at least retain its current value. He needed to know that Nicole and Jesse would know exactly how much they had to live on. And once the $750,000 of life insurance was added, they would have some years to stabilize. There was no way he was going to put them in a position where that $800,000 was reduced to $400,000 because of market volatility. Gold would guarantee his family would at least have enough leeway to survive his passing.

"You're making a big mistake," his advisor said in a tone of entitlement. The advisor had been acting aloof and extremely condescending since Stan arrived. Stan had other, more important things on his mind, or he would have torn into the broker full force sooner than he did.

"No, Barry, *you* made a big mistake. You kept me in these positions and watched me lose 60 percent in value. You

CHAPTER FIVE: THE CODE

just sat and watched me. What's to say this $800,000 won't go to $400,000 next? Answer that question, Barry."

"Stan."

"Saying my name won't make things better. Please stop saying my name. Tell me this, Barry," Stan said sarcastically, "How can you guarantee I won't lose more?"

"Well, I can't," Barry answered.

"Exactly. I know you can't, but I know what can. Gold. Or better said, gold gives me a fighting chance. At least gold respects my principal."

"But if you buy gold, you won't keep up with inflation," Barry responded. "I've told you this a million times, and yet you don't want to hear it."

"Seriously? Are you out of your mind?" Stan asked in honest confusion. "You're telling me to worry about inflation?"

"Let me get my manager," Barry suggested, rising from his chair. "He can explain this better than I can."

"Muck your manager, and muck his manager," Stan snapped. He would frequently substitute profanity by one letter so you could still get the point. "I'll tell you what you can get –my money."

Barry sat back down.

Stan stood up.

He was trying to maintain a tone of voice appropriate for the professional office environment, but the quieter he became, the more intense his voice got. He looked Barry right in the eyes, and tried to be as transparent as possible.

"Look at me, Barry. I'm dying."

Barry's eyes widened.

"I have to do what is in the best interest of my family. How dare you bring up inflation when I've just lost more than half my net worth? How does losing 60 percent in eighteen months keep up with inflation? How does that work? And how does that protect my family when I'm gone?"

Barry grew pale, but didn't answer. He swallowed heavily, looking at the door behind Stan.

"It doesn't help my family; that much is clear. But I know it would help you if I stayed, wouldn't it? You want to make more money, more commissions off of my account. An account that you put on the wrong path, because you didn't want to recommend common sense investments that were best for me, but not best for you. Why do all investments have to sound difficult and complicated? Because it makes it sound like you're worth the money. I'm learning this late, but I've learned it now, Barry. I've learned it now."

Stan put both hands up in frustration, and then softened his voice. "Barry, man, you could have put 15 percent of my portfolio in physical gold like I asked years ago, and still made a commission off my other positions. And I wouldn't have lost my backside. But you talked me out of it, and the worst part is that I *let* you talk me out of it. I did the work, I made the money, and to be honest, you haven't done spit but help me lose it!"

Stan took a black pen from the inner pocket of his jacket, bent down, and signed the paperwork on the small table beside him. He grabbed his bag.

"I expect every penny in my account to be out of your firm in twenty-four hours." He turned and walked out the door, got into his car, and drove away.

***

The radio grew fuzzy for a moment, and then came in strong and clear. (Radio Announcer)

CHAPTER FIVE: THE CODE

"In business news, the DOW is in a free fall today as consumer confidence numbers are lower than expected, indicating most Americans feel the economic storm has yet to end," the announcer said.

Stan reached for the radio, cutting it off with a quick twist. But one phrase stuck with him, 'economic storm.'

Interesting they put it in those terms, He thought.

An 'economic storm' is a very revealing concept. Storms don't ask for permission; they destroy everything in their path, and have no consideration for whether you're prepared or not. So if an economic storm has the same characteristics as a natural one, what can withstand natural storms? When the rain has stopped, and the floods have rolled back, what do you see? You only see foundations. The tree limbs may be gone, but the stump doesn't move; the house may have blown away but the foundation on which it stood doesn't budge. Economic storms blow away anything not firmly planted.

"That's just what gold is," Stan began to ponder. "It's a financial foundation. Gold doesn't fade away; it doesn't budge in a storm. Why don't I have gold in my portfolio? This is crazy." Just then, his thoughts went back to what he'd heard from Dr. Angelo.

He saw his exit in the rear view mirror and decided to jump on Texas Highway 130 and take the longer, more scenic route home. The day was beautiful. The sun was shining so brightly, paying no attention to the human pain beneath it. Everything was changing rapidly. In a very short period of time, circumstances had pushed a man, already decisive in all his ways, to be even more purposeful. He knew what he had to do, and he knew he had to do it now. It was time to stop losing. He wasn't concerned with net gain at this point; he wanted to get out of the negative and back to zero. Zero was the new profit. It was time to call Paul.

P. Madison

Paul Madison was his friend – which is a miracle all unto itself. Paul doesn't have friends, but somehow over the last ten years he and Stan had established a relationship, an odd one, but a relationship nonetheless. Stan was about to call on that relationship for some help.

A fifty seven-year old retired businessman, Paul had the unique ability to assess the strategic, business, social and psychological elements of any given situation. He'd spent 35 years in the capital markets, funding mezzanine startups. Today, his net worth was north of $100 million – way north. These days, his time was spent on a one hundred acre farm outside of Austin. In clear terms, Paul is mean. His intellect, money, accomplishments and world-view is far elevated above even the most educated, and he lets you know it. People who accuse him of being arrogant are being too kind; he is obnoxious at a celestial level.

Paul believes he is a deity. If he met the Pope, he would say, "I'm Paul, who are you?" He is authentically fake, that is to say his rough outer edge and noticeable discontent for every other living thing comes naturally. He is dreadfully blind to anyone else's concerns but his own. To see Paul from a distance is to notice the partitions of his hair. He isn't losing his hair; he pulls it out on his own. He's a walking horror scene, a Hollywood set. No one looks like this. Paul's a frightening ghost. Add to this the facts that Paul wears washed out clothes of no specific color, uses his face to lead his body into a room, and carries a look that's stuck on confusion.

CHAPTER FIVE: THE CODE

During his career in the capital markets, he was known for walking around the office saying to people, "We need to talk." Just for the tension such words create. Paul never *needs* to talk about anything, but he got joy in lighting anxiety in the people so he could sit back and watch them squirm around the possibility of potential confrontation; a dictator even in common conversation.

But Stan had learned to tolerate Paul's abrasive personality because he always learned something powerful every time they spoke. Stan set up a meeting at a local coffee house frequented by both men. Stan walked in the door and saw his unfriendly friend sitting at the third table against the back wall. Stan waved as he approached.
"Good morning, Paul."
Paul ignored Stan and instead motioned to the server to refresh his coffee that had been refreshed only sixty seconds earlier. Paul doesn't respond to anybody until he's ready.
"No long pants today, huh?" Paul referenced Stan's shorts as if long pants had some aristocratic meaning and shorts a thing of peasantry.
Stan looked down at his shorts, trying to figure out what was the problem, and then remembered this is how Paul likes each conversation – he wants you to start off doubting yourself from the word 'go.' Stan smiled and started right in on why he was there.
"I've just moved my accounts."
Paul laughed.
"Finally got tired of the bullshit?" Paul responded.
"Yeah, it's way past time. I've lost so much and I know from my own research and the books you gave me that I didn't have to lose. I *did not* have to lose."
"Well – you did," Paul said.

Stan's eyebrows asked Paul how he came to that conclusion.

"No matter how many books, how many conversations we've had – until you lose what *you've* worked so hard for, you just don't understand the importance of taking control of your own finances. Understand this, those selling you financial products at most financial firms have a superior skill set over those who don't want to be sold. Think of is this way; most financial firms are bodybuilders who are rapists and the general investing public is a one hundred pound college girl – who, at midnight, just accepted a ride home."

"Wow."

"Get it now?" Paul asked.

"I do."

"It's pure physics, 'interpersonal physics,' as I call it. Whoever has the greatest ability to manipulate logic wins the thinking battle every time. And the greatest manipulation of logic is transforming logic into emotions.

"Explain that," Stan said.

"Ok, I sold billions of dollars' worth of deals to investors, private equity, venture capitalists, etc. Ninety percent of the deals were shit. But it didn't matter. I understood the investor better than he understood himself so I always had the upper hand. In fact, the only opposition to me was me. I would argue with myself about whether to get $15 million from the person sitting in front of me or $20 million. The investor was irrelevant. They hadn't the intellectual tools to compete. Yes, many of them had Ph.Ds. from major institutions and alphabet soup behind their names, which usually only served to make them dumber and dumber. Wall Street is designed for people like that. Wall Street is designed to take advantage of two types of people, the smart dummy and the dumb dummy. And the tool they use to pry money out of your hands, at the

CHAPTER FIVE: THE CODE

most fundamental level – is words. Words make money, not people."

Paul continued, "If your life is ever going to change, it's going to be because you understand how language, how words effect people. Fuck everything else. When you know how to properly communicate, you can do absolutely anything. Most people use words to describe; I use words to create. There is a slight difference of about $100 million between the two approaches.

Very early in my career, I learned that after I stopped concentrating on MBA shit like writing business plans, which by the way is for dummies, and I started concentrating on learning how people operate, everything changed. If I lost everything tomorrow and was flat broke on the street with $5 in my pocket, give me three years and I'll be writing a book about how I turned $5 into $100 million again. Great communicators can tell you to go to hell and make you feel good about your trip there. Actually, it's scary stuff. But few people have that skill, and those that do, have the skill at different levels of potency. One guy is good raising money at the $100,000 level but his psychology won't let him operate at the $10 million level. The economy of scale applies to personality as much as money. So much of financial success is simply about boldness and the average person is basically timid."

As Paul spoke, Stan took copious notes, heading one column *"Psychology of Words"* and the other, *"The History."* In the margins, he jotted memorable anecdotes used to underscore both points.

Words
In the margins, he wrote the following examples, recording in shorthand anecdotes he didn't want to risk forgetting.

Paul explained how power is big, money is big, but words are bigger. A $30,000 per year salaried police officer can walk up to Bill Gates and place him under arrest like a petty thief if the little piece of paper in his hand reads 'warrant.' The law is bigger than money, yet the law can only be expressed using words. That is why once you learn how to effectively communicate you are actually learning how to make 'laws' in people's heads. People generally want to follow the law and so they will follow you.

Words are law. Ninety-nine percent of the world doesn't understand this; people are followers. I followed the advice of Barry for no other reason but that he told me to. In fact, all of the evidence pointed away from following his investment advice. I followed still. I realized now that Barry never asked me what I wanted. *Interesting.* When someone asks you for something, this is the first indicator they are not operating under a 'law' mentality because the law doesn't ask anything. The law states what will happen if *this* or what will happen if *that*. The law is unshakably confident. It needs no opinion to validate its position. Laws of wealth are very similar to natural laws. When is the last time the sun asked you if it could shine?

Notes in margin: Today proves once again that it's worth it to deal with the extremely offensive man sitting in front of me. He has real insight.

CHAPTER FIVE: THE CODE

Stan came out of his mental fog and began to process Paul's voice again. "...Wall Street is trained to speak in a quotable style; I know because I trained many of them," Paul said. "Your words become your charisma. Your language can create soldiers in the field who market what you say in your absence. Your words argue for you even when you are nowhere around. I used to teach a morning class to young brokers based on the following communication principles; Phrasing, Attribution, and something I call 'Quote speaking.'

In short, these classes emphasized three points. When selling investors, you must first succinctly assemble your phrases in advance of saying them. Thinking beforehand is much more valuable than thinking on the spot. Second, eliminate personal attribution when speaking (I think, I believe). Can you imagine Patrick Henry saying, 'I think give me liberty or give me death?'

Thirdly, express your thoughts as if you are reading a great historical quote. The power of quoting isn't that the person being quoted was so wise, but rather that they are present for you to attack. Ideas, no matter how bad they are, seem unassailable when the originator of the idea isn't saying it. For example, let's say I was looking to get you invested to the tune of $5 million in a private equity vehicle. Let's say the company makes trinkets that go on top of larger trinkets that reduce the odor of cat shit. Now, I can either tell you how much my personal cat named Pussy loves the pleasant smell of fresh linen trinkets – or I can tell you how much some famous billionaire in the Cayman Islands just bought $100 million worth of the company's stock. Whenever you reference belief, success or wisdom to a third person more successful party, people bite. It's really that simple. I mean really, if I told you what Warren Buffett says about a particular investment, even if you disagreed, you'll probably keep it to yourself mostly because the momentum of the universe says Buffett is right and you're wrong. This is the fundamental premise that keeps the investing public scared to follow their gut; most believe somebody else knows better."

Noticing Stan had his head down and was writing feverishly, Paul still needed to make sure all his attention was totally devoted to him.
"Hope you're getting all of this cause I'm not repeating myself." Paul said.
"I got it."
Paul continued, "Now, I say all that to say this, Wall Street isn't only fast-talking bull-shitters; that's pedestrian, bush league, that's psychology at the $100,000 level I spoke about before, car salesman fodder. People who really know how to communicate a story, these kinds of people say very little and can generate hundreds of millions of dollars. The ultimate irony is, those who best communicate, don't have to say much. When I used to make phone calls to prospective investors, I used a special method."
"What was special about it?" Stan asked.
"It worked. That's special, isn't it?" Paul asked.
"Yes," Stan answered.
Paul shook his head. "When the investor picked up the phone, I would do three things. First, I would ask them if they could hear me; they would say 'yes.' This is important because of momentum. I want the listener to hear himself say 'yes.' I want him to know he's capable of saying 'yes.' I want him to feel the vibration of the word running across his teeth. Second, I would immediately apologize for the limited time I have on the phone. This establishes the value of what I'm about to say before I say it. It lets the listener know there is an

CHAPTER FIVE: THE CODE

urgency, an expiration on the opportunity I am presenting. Third, I would recall a familiar event. For example, if the potential investor had already spoken with another colleague, I would reference that conversation so that..."

Stan forced his way into the conversation, "So how does this relate to discouraging people from buying gold and other valuable commodities?"

"Will you shut the fuck up? Will you?" Paul asked in a moment of instant intensity, appearing out of nowhere. As he reached for and touched a pain in his lower back, he motioned for his server to refresh his coffee and continued as if Stan asked nothing, as if his words were but passing gnats.

"The street understands that if they say something, it becomes true. They understand language in its purest form. Whether a story is true or not is more irrelevant than beetle dung. Wall Street creates premise. They create their own foundation and when you own the foundation, you can build whatever you want on it, tear it down, and build something else. You can put somebody in jail for selling junk bonds, and then create the same thing by a different name and call it "Triple C" paper. When you own the premise, you can lock somebody up for selling properties that don't exist, but then from watching and analyzing where they went wrong, you can create credit default swaps on companies that do exist and make billions. Wall Street took the concept of 'technically backed' securities, which is a contradiction on its face. Wall Street then delivered this concept to the investing public in the form of an electronic dream - better known as an ETF. The ETF came out like they were fresh and new. And that's the power of story. Every Wall Street financial product is built upon a previous crime that just needed to be tweaked in order to become legal."

"Wait a minute, are you saying...?"

THE PREMISE, THE MONEY & THE GOLD

"I'm saying what I said. Don't interrupt me." Paul said and took a sip of coffee.

"Gold or silver are two of the smartest investments on this planet we call earth. It's not even up for debate. If you look where gold was 10 years ago and where gold is now, and compare it to where the DOW was 10 years ago and where the DOW now, you have to ask yourself a question. Who is benefitting by the general public staying out of physical gold? Who is feeding this story of gold being speculative, one of the firmest, most dependable, globally respected forms of real value in the world? Who is doing that? I'll answer for you."

"This thing is getting shallow!" Paul yelled at his server, holding his coffee in one hand and pointing to it with his opposite index finger.

"When the average American owns gold, the entire monetary system is thrown off. Banks and the Wall Street complex would much rather you put your money in a CD versus buying bullion. I had a client who was making 0.056% in his money market account on a $500,000 balance. So I started thinking – hell, I'll take the money for him and I'll pay 1% interest on it, personally, out of my pocket. I could literally make more money paying him double. I could at least pull 3% off those same funds and keep 2%. So why didn't he think about that? Because simple answers don't make sense. Banks and Wall Street operate on capital ratios and leverage. Banks are unbelievably powerful. Every day, banks take on deposit the thing people live and die for – money. Think about that for a moment. You spend ninety percent of your life trying to get your hands on these worthless pieces of paper we call money. Then we take this stuff into a building and give it to somebody who says it'll be here when you get back. It's some funny shit, but only when you really think about it, which is the fundamental problem, nobody thinks about it."

CHAPTER FIVE: THE CODE

"Ever crossed a bank?" Paul asked in a rare moment of dialogue share.

"Once I did," answered Stan.

"What did they do?"

"They closed my account." Stan answered.

Paul reared back and laughed heartily as if Stan had just given a punch line to a joke.

"I'm laughing because that's happened to me so many times. Banks are like bloodhounds in heat; they smell everything. If they even remotely think you're doing anything that in some imaginative world encroaches upon what they think they're comfortable with, they just close your account. It's unreal." Paul said.

"I distinctly remember one week back at the firm when a bank gave it to us with thorns. Our payroll that week was $135,000, and for no reason at all, aside from the fact that they knew we dealt in private equity, and that wasn't their issue *by the way*, they closed the account. They didn't like the precious metals side of our business. They hated it because it made my firm look too much like a financial institution, and no one takes that title but them. So right in the middle of payroll, I got a call saying my account was closed and that they would cut me a check for my $200,000 balance in about thirty days."

"What did you do?" Stan asked.

"I made some calls and had to borrow the money and pay it back with shark-like interest. Banks don't care. That should be their motto. They should stick it right on the window next to FDIC, which I always say means 'Fuck Depositors Ignorant Cunts.' But I digress."

"Wow."

"Back to my point, when you put your money in a bank, that same bank's investment division leverages those funds up to one-hundred times or more on Wall Street. You, the perpetual depositor, provides certainty of future revenues for the bank, and because they're keeping your return at half a percent on a CD, they can make money or lose money knowing that the aggregate of such profit or loss will never prevent them for paying you your measly .056%. What do you think all that P/E ratio, EBITDA, alpha, beta, and book value bullshit is? It's bullshit. Old man Charlie Munger said every time you see the word 'EBITDA', you should substitute the word 'bullshit.' I love Munger.

The people I was pitching years ago weren't just pawns in a game I controlled, but rather a game I created, and custom fit just for them, just for their mentality, just for the gaps in their understanding. That's exactly what your advisor has done to you all these years – he played your gaps. And your greatest gap is your confidence or the lack thereof. You had the same information on precious metals investing ten years ago. The information hasn't changed, you have."

"Shit," moaned Stan.

"You are correct," Paul responded. "Playing the gap is some profitable shit – at least for your advisor, it was."

Look, if I was sitting in front of a guy named 'Jim,' I could be more 'Jim' than he could. I could morph and understand his thoughts, his demeanor, and leverage the psychology of the sale against his own interests. I remember we once had a client named David Goodenuff. That was his real name. We had a running bet at the firm on how many times we could say 'good enough' while pitching him an investment without him catching on. He was a degenerate money-sender. He would send ten grand to anybody who called him just to say 'hello, Mr. Goodenuff.' He loved a story, so we gave him story; you know, we wanted to make our customers happy," Paul said with a smirk.

CHAPTER FIVE: THE CODE

"It did not matter what the investment was. If you called him, he'd send money. We'd call him and say, 'David, listen, I know the 14% you saw in your last return may be good enough for you, but it's not good enough for us over here. We want you to make more. Then we would speak to ourselves in rhetorical fashion as if he weren't even on the dammed phone. We'd say, 'So what is good enough for us?' And then we would proceed to tell him about the unbelievable investment we were about to sell starting 'tomorrow' and, if he wanted us to, we would call him first before anyone else. These are the basic principles that control human nature. We all want to be liked; we want to be in the 'in' group, whatever the fuck that means. We don't want to sit and watch everyone else make money. It's like investors run around like three year olds saying, 'me, me, me – pick me please - I wanna play.'"

Stan sat across the table feeling depressed and empowered at the same time – empowered that he now understood what had been going on all these years, but depressed that he just discovered, or rather accepted the answers that were so obvious before. He hated that his life could have been better if only he'd listened to his gut. He still hadn't told Paul about his medical condition.

***

Paul glanced down at the $50,000 Rolex sitting on his wrist like a scoop of Häagen-Dazs.

"Time to go ride the horses," he said.

"And by the way Stan, don't feel bad, well actually, do feel bad; you lost half your money," Paul said. "Now, the question is, what are you going to do to get it back? The same trench used to get you further away from your money is still there. You can turn around and follow that same trench right back to your money. That's what you need to understand. The same road that takes you from Austin to Atlanta is the same road that takes you from Atlanta to Austin. Don't give up, just turn around."

Stan had been taking notes the entire time, notes on his color-coordinated pad. Two hours had passed and Paul had covered every aspect of how the sales machine in the financial markets works, how this sales machine has nothing to do with logic, but everything to do with story, everything to do with emotions. He'd recalled real-life examples of unbelievable approaches to selling stocks, and real estate that the general public has no defense against. Stan got what he came for - wisdom.

It was time to go, and their server seemed so happy they were leaving that she almost gave *them* a tip.

As they walked out, Stan couldn't help but appreciate the material results of Paul's career and the luxuries that only knowledge well-executed can bring. He lived on a one hundred acre ranch on some of the most expensive property right outside of Austin. Paul climbed into his custom classic Mustang and put the top down. Stan walked up to the driver's side window. He was going to tell him about his condition and the prognosis for his future.

"Good seeing you Paul, thanks so much for the information – you know I didn't get a chance to tell you…"

In mid-sentence, Paul revved his engine and sped off without even looking in Stan's direction.

Stan stood behind the Mustang-induced dust cloud thinking of how to make his financial comeback. At this

CHAPTER FIVE: THE CODE

point, he was gluttonous for information. He needed to learn or relearn everything fast. There was little time for conjecture. He had an idea.

Stan started his car and reached for a CD in the glove box that had been sitting there since Paul gave it to him two months prior. He hit play and the narrator began to speak.

Chapter Six
THE HISTORY OF MONEY

CHAPTER SIX: THE HISTORY OF MONEY

THE HISTORY OF MONEY IS A LURID ONE. There is a reason for this. The mind is a circus; you can find everything there. The good and the forbidden constantly flirt in the mind. But this flirting, this caressing still needs a catalyst, an irresistible motive to reach its deepest, darkest corners. And nothing will make people, even those afraid of the dark, walk into a haunted house like this *one thing*. This *one thing* can push men of good will to consummate with evil. Money.

Money causes odd things to happen. People marry, steal, plot, scheme and even kill to get their hands on it. But money is only a tool; it only helps you fix things. Most view money as an end instead of a means to get there. To get it, people will do things they would never have done under any other circumstances. The world revolves around money, period. Though it rarely happens in the western world, people in other countries regularly starve to death or die of thirst or exposure for lack of money.

It's no wonder we become obsessed with it. Why, then, do we let our money move beyond our control? Why, when this is one of the most important things to our survival, do we put our trust in someone else, fail to do our own research, and allow the person controlling our money to ignore our suggestions? Why do we ignore our own gut feelings? Money becomes one of the most important facts of maintaining the lifestyle we've come to know, especially during retirement, when the income flow stops. Yet so many people choose to leave their retirement funds in the hands of others, and trust that those others will do what's best. People believe what the media tells them about the best ways to invest that money, and the issues to avoid. In short, they buy into the story.

Wall Street leads them in the wrong direction and the economy goes downhill; it means thousands of people lose millions of dollars. And yet the public continues to believe. Why? *Because they are trained them to believe.*

Wall Street can't maintain power if people stop believing in it. The bankers and brokers won't make the money they're used to making, and will lose the control they're used to. So Wall Street and its media partners do their best to control the public's thinking. They encourage stocks and bonds, and push the traditional brokerages. They tell people to trust them. They downplay things like precious metals – gold, silver, and the like – by telling the public that those are speculative, rather than 'guaranteed' value. They, in turn, maintain control of precious metals for themselves.

Government prudence

Like every system in nature, the system of money is based on hierarchy. Someone somewhere has the upper hand on something everybody needs. If we were talking about corn, the corn farmer has the upper hand. If we're talking about fresh water, the water treatment company has the upper hand, and if we're talking about money, the upper hand goes to government.

'Government' is an interesting word if you take away its connotation and stick to definition only. When you stick to definition, the word 'government' is quite prudent; it is quite safe. I know; prudence and safety just don't remind you of government, but think of this. When you rent a U-Haul trailer to move five hundred miles out of state, you'll notice something. The U-Haul truck has a governor. This governor keeps you from going over a specific speed for the reasons of safety and prudence. This governor protects others from you and you from yourself. This governor elevates the probability that you will arrive at your destination without incident. This is 'government' at its finest. But remember that circus we spoke about?

CHAPTER SIX: THE HISTORY OF MONEY

Now imagine you're driving down the highway on that same trip. What if the company in charge of placing that governor in the U-Haul engine was paid by the state to 'forget' to install it? Let's say the state's reasoning may have been so its law enforcement division can write more tickets, thereby funding new roads and bridges – in other words, good agendas mixed with evil methodology. As you travel down a Tennessee mountain with an extra ten thousand pounds, you notice what was 60 MPH five minutes earlier is now 90 MPH.

You hit the brakes.

Nothing happens.

You hit the brakes again. Screeching metal responds but your speed only increases.

Your pores instantly burst with sweat.

The uninstalled governor has now presented an even bigger problem because the brakes on your U-Haul, designed to stop a truck of a certain weight, weren't designed to stop a truck with an extra ten thousand pounds of weight and no governor.

At the end of the highway decline, you see a school bus stopped, its lights blinking.

Children are walking across the road in a straight line.

You pump the brakes again . . . nothing.

Although atheist, you begin to pray.

Out of the corner of your eye, you catch glimpse of a path veering off to the side – looks like a pebble beach on an incline – it's an emergency turn-off.

You take a hard right and, at full speed, your U-Haul truck buries itself into the only thing keeping you from the de-boarding school kids.

You come to a violent stop at the top of the ramp.

Your front axle teeters over the top of the hill.

Scared and confused, you thank the God you've never spoken to. And all of this happens because somebody wanted a little more *money*. That, my friend, is the runaway nature of modern government. Government puts you in danger and then legislates that an emergency ramp be built to protect you. Government makes money on both sides of every event.

But it gets even more complicated because government doesn't even want your money. That is correct; ultimately, government isn't after your money. Money is only the transportation to get them where they really want to go. Remember, the state paid the installation company to remove the safety precaution so the state could write more tickets so it could make more money to do 'good.' This happens at the state and federal level all the time. But wait, why would the entity that exclusively owns the right to print money, do something for money? Would a fish buy a bottle of water from you? Well – yes, not because the fish needs water, but because the fish needs influence. And this is the circus, the sideshow.

What government proposes to need, it does not. But the appearance of this need creates what government really wants, the power of influence, the influence to have the general population believe paper money is what they should strive for. The influence to create positive premise for a currency that is constitutionally bastardly. The influence to deceive.

Value

Paper money has no inherent value. Money is odd that way. There is nothing you can do with money. You can't eat it, it can't keep you warm, and *it* doesn't cure anything. The only purpose of paper money is to bring something of actual value into your life. Paper money is just an arrow on a piece of paper; all it does is point. If tomorrow morning you woke up and found the new form of payment for all debts was grasshoppers, within the hour, you'd see people running

CHAPTER SIX: THE HISTORY OF MONEY

in the streets turning over rocks to find grasshoppers. Well-dressed men and women would walk into stores with the squeezed out lime-colored juices from the grasshoppers all over their clothes. Paper money is the grasshopper of our time – but nothing has ever or will ever replace gold because gold is the earth's original asset. Before monetary policy, before the Federal Reserve, before Wall Street, there was gold. Gold doesn't have value; gold *is* value.

So how does an entire country change the very definition of money to something with no inherent value? How do you go from solid gold to thin pieces of paper backed by nothing but the word of government – the same government who makes money on both sides of every event? You do this by changing the collective narrative. When you change the narrative, good people and criminals alike, both seek the same thing. No one walks up to a man in the street, presses the cold tip of a gun into his side and says "Give me your gold!" Everybody wants paper money, but unfortunately, most have no idea it isn't worth much at all.

Early in the country's history, the US government realized that it was unnecessary and inconvenient for its citizens to carry pieces of gold with them everywhere they went. What's more, they realized gold pieces could be difficult to 'measure' – how much was each piece worth? What if the goods you were buying weren't expensive enough to cost your entire chunk of gold? With the invention of the printing press, the government had a new route – they printed national 'currency' in the form of paper money, gave it denominations, and secured its value with its own stock of gold. Each piece of paper money was guaranteed by the government; if a citizen wanted to go trade it in for gold, they could theoretically do so.

The money itself, though, was only worth the paper on which it was printed; *unless the government guaranteed it.*

This is the honor system on which paper currency is built. The government tells us that each piece of paper is worth a specific amount, and maintains the printing rights itself. As its citizens, we believe government is telling the truth, and use paper money in trade and commerce.

But how do we maintain this trust? If we begin to question things too closely, or even ask for proof, what do we do if we find fault in the government's word of honor? In the 1930s, during the Great Depression, President Roosevelt forced the public to turn its gold over to the government, to shore up the government's store of gold and control the price. Citizens were given paper money for their gold stocks, but lost control of some of their financial destiny. Without physical gold, they controlled very little value. They became dependent on the government's word that the paper money was worth something. Roosevelt didn't intend for this to be the first step toward distrust, but it started a landslide.

In the 1970s, trust was further derailed. Nixon took the US dollar off the gold standard, which means that the government no longer guaranteed each dollar with a piece of gold. Now citizens were even more dependent on the government's word. Since then, the US government has been selling its gold on the international market to keep the price of gold down, while printing paper money at an alarming rate, to pay its bills. The US dollar falls in value as it becomes more common, and falls in confidence as it draws further away from gold.

And yet the public continues to trust. When will that bubble burst? And what will the public do when it's left holding pieces of paper that it finds to be worthless?

The answer is simple: hold gold as the only thing with

set value, and maintain your worth. Hold the thing that the US government finds so valuable, and trust something solid rather than something built on hot air.

Gold vs. Paper Money Narrative

Most people don't think twice about money, except to worry about the fact they don't have enough or wish they had more to buy the things they really want. However, they don't really consider the actual money itself or from where it came.

In the beginning – obviously – there was no money. Finding something to eat and having shelter was the most important business of life. People banded together as tribes to hunt for animals and gather plants and berries. That's right, the old hunter-gatherer tribes. Eventually, they figured out how to plant the leftover seeds from dinner and grow crops. This developed into agriculture and people branched out into other various specialty activities, which meant people were no longer completely self-sufficient. That meant they needed a way to exchange the surplus corn or cows for things they did not have or could not produce themselves, such as metal cookware.

This meant trade, or *bartering*, where someone exchanged their goods for the goods from another person or tribe. The only problem was figuring out how many pans a cow would buy or how much corn was needed to buy a single frying pan. What people needed was a *medium of exchange*, a material that could be passed between buyer and seller to complete transactions and pay for things of value. Remember, paper money bring things of value into your life; it is the medium, not the value.

A medium of exchange is also the precise definition of *currency*; seashells, tulip bulbs, gold, and paper money are forms of currency and have been used in the past or are still in use. Gold has been used down through the ages because of its *intrinsic* value, or value all on its own, without any governmental authority having to set that value, as opposed to paper money which is called a *fiat* currency because the value is set by a declaration, a fiat; a narrative.

Historically, transactions conducted in gold were never in doubt; the only problem was that carrying gold was inconvenient because it became bulkier and heavier the larger the purchase. It was also dangerous because it was hard to hide and its value made its owners targets for robbery. Slowly, a system developed which largely concerned the rich because the poor up until the last 100 years possessed very little actual money. They continued to survive by producing their own food whenever possible and bartering for the other items they were unable to make themselves. However, the wealthy began to accumulate gold and they took it to goldsmiths to have it fashioned into jewelry and other objects of public prestige.

However, they would also return to the goldsmith if they needed money. After awhile, certain enterprising goldsmiths in England and Germany figured out that rather than handing back the gold, they could sign a note that said the customer had a certain amount of gold stored with the goldsmith. This note could be given to merchants and other sellers of goods, who could then come to the goldsmith and collect the gold. Or the ownership of the gold could be signed over to the new owner and left with the goldsmith.

These notes became known as *promissory notes* because they promised the *bearer*, or the person possessing the note, he or she could collect the weight in gold printed on the note. Through the creation of this simple transaction, the goldsmiths created the world's first banks. Today's checks and cash are both forms of promissory notes. Checks are promissory notes made by individuals that they will pay out money kept in their individual checking accounts. Cash, which is formally called *bank notes*, are promissory notes, where the bank promises to pay the bearer. The natural question in the economy of today is: "Pay what?" How or why would a bank pay the bearer of cash with more cash? They don't. That will be explained momentarily. However, under the system originated by the goldsmiths, the bearer of cash was entitled to the amount gold printed on the bank note. So, for example, in the United States of many years ago, the owner of a 10-dollar bill could go to a US mint and receive 10 dollars in actual gold.

Money in Colonial America

The banking system that evolved from the goldsmiths of Europe eventually traveled west with the European colonists to America. The true story of money in America is complex because it has always been a story of competing monetary systems. When the English came, they naturally brought with them their English money, which would seem like it would be the beginning and end of money in America until the American Revolution. Yet that's not what happened. The reason is that colonies are never created to be equal to the mother country – on purpose. They are set up as economic 'machines' designed to transfer the raw materials and natural resources of the colony back to the mother country as rapidly as possible at the lowest possible price.

Silver, the metal on which the British money was based, was counted by the mother country as one of those natural resources. Laws were actually passed banning the export of silver coins to the colonies to attempt to ensure the mother country got it all. As a result, British money became very scarce in the colonies. So the colonists began using money from other colonial powers, including Spanish American silver coins from Mexico and Peru, the Portuguese cruzado, the French ecu, and the ducatoon from Holland, to make their purchases.

The eight reales, or 'piece of eight' coin, was the highest value Spanish silver coin found in the Western Hemisphere. It was also one of the most popular in the Colonies and the first coin to be called a 'dollar' in the English Colonies, from the Dutch word 'daalder,' which was a corruption of the German word 'thaler,' yet another form of money also found in Colonial America.

Conversion of these coins was a nightmare because each of the 13 colonies had its own exchange rate for every kind of currency. Even British coins were not worth the same in the colonies as they were in the home country. Paper money redeemable in coins was also used in different places throughout the colonies, but it never lasted very long for reasons that will be explained a bit later. This was largely the story of money in America until the advent of the American Revolution.

Made In America

Other than the Boston Mint, formed in 1652 and lasting 30 years, no other substantial or serious attempt was made to coin money in America, largely because the English Crown forbade it. This became a real problem, especially when those fateful shots were exchanged at Lexington and Concord in 1775 that brought on the American Revolution.

CHAPTER SIX: THE HISTORY OF MONEY

The new government was broke and it needed money to field the ragtag bunch of militia and citizen soldiers known as the Continental Army in its bid to win against the most professional army on earth at the time, the British Army.

There was little or no gold or silver available to coin money, so the Continental Congress printed its own paper money called the 'Continental.'

Of course, it wasn't long before the British found out about the new money and sabotaged it by printing thousands of counterfeits. That, as much as spending by the Revolutionary government, was the main reason that anything worthless was deemed 'not worth a Continental.' Overprinting of paper bank notes was also the reason all the other paper money schemes tried in the past had also failed.

However, the Continental was not the exclusive 'national' money. Again, think of competing currencies. The individual colonies were also printing their own money. All of these were fiat currencies. And, those foreign coins were still bouncing around in circulation. The Spanish reale was officially recognized as *legal tender*, or official money in the US, all the way until 1857. No significant attempts were made to coin money during the war.

What happened after the war always gets glossed over by the history books. There's the surrender at Yorktown in 1781 and suddenly there's a Constitution and everyone has dollar bills in their pockets. Nothing could be further from the truth. What gets obscured almost completely is the Articles of Confederation, which was our national government for eight years from 1781 to 1789.

Our first president was technically not George Washington, but John Hanson and there were seven others because each one only served a year each. Washington was actually the first president under the Constitution, beginning in 1789.

107

And of course, the topic of money *after* the Continental is not usually discussed at all, probably because it's not easily summarized in a couple of sentences. Unlike the government under the Constitution, which is a *federation* with a stronger central government, the Articles established a confederation in which the central government was weaker and the states were stronger. The result for the monetary system was there was no publicly-issued national currency.

All money was printed and minted by the individual states. Minting coins, also called *specie*, by the states was relatively modest in the forms of small denominations and in non-precious metals such as copper. Although individuals attempted to mint gold or silver coins, none were minted in amounts sufficient to be put into circulation by any state government.

Chapter Seven
THE BANK

CHAPTER SEVEN: THE BANK

IN 1780, THE YEAR BEFORE THE AMERICAN REVOLUTION ENDED, a move was made that began a debate that raged throughout the history of the American nation and, to a certain extent, up until the present day. The result is that it split the monetary supply in two: public and private. Public money is that which was minted or printed by the national and state government; private money was what was issued by America's first bank, the Bank of Pennsylvania. However, the Superintendent of Finance Robert Morris succeeded in pushing the Congress of the Confederation—the old Continental Congress—into chartering a bank. As a result, the Bank of Pennsylvania became the Bank of North America, a privately-owned bank that printed bank notes that were legal tender. Morris backed the currency with gold and silver he had borrowed from the Netherlands and France and with profits obtained from his war-related businesses.

The stated reason for creating the bank was to improve the credit worthiness of the United States in the eyes of the world and make it easier for the new government to borrow money. Morris and his young protégé, a young Army officer named Alexander Hamilton, wanted the bank to be the sole depository of the national governments money and its only issuer of currency. However, the Pennsylvania legislature saw this as a threat and yanked the bank's charter in 1785. Morris would succeed in getting the charter reinstated two years later, but the Bank of North America was dead. Neither Morris nor Hamilton accepted this as a defeat. They watched and waited until the time was right.

In the meantime, the states began granting charters for banks all over the country. With or without enough gold or silver backing them up, these banks made loans and printed money that was all legal tender in the United States.

The Constitutional-Currency Connection

Shays' Rebellion is the usual reason given as to why the Articles of Confederation were replaced with the Constitution. The rebellion flared in Massachusetts and under the Articles, there was no national army. Under the Articles, the president had to convince the states to send troops to put down the rebellion. They did, but the relatively slow speed of the response was interpreted as a failure of the entire Articles of Confederation and the reason that it needed to be replaced.

However, the root causes of Shays' Rebellion were never really addressed. Namely, creditors were seizing the houses, farms, and walking straight into houses to seize the belongings of Daniel Shays and the other Revolutionary War veterans who were unable to plant the crops that would pay their bills because they were away fighting for the country. Instead of intervening as a national government to protect the veterans and mediate a solution, a push was made to create a stronger national system of government that would have the strength and power to 'shoot now and ask questions later', if at all. This new system would create a national court system, which would strengthen the power of creditors to collect from debtors.

The proponents of this stronger, centralized government were called Federalists, and chief among those Federalists were Hamilton and Morris. Patrick 'give me liberty or give me death' Henry said he "smelled a rat" in response to the upcoming Constitutional Convention. Jefferson was conveniently neutralized in France where he was serving as an ambassador. He didn't hear about the Constitution until after its adoption.

James Madison and others bought the argument that a new stronger Constitution was needed. They finished their work in 1787 and by 1789, all of the states had ratified it.

The Constitution called for the minting of coins, but to this day, it makes no mention of the government ever printing any money. Minting coins was not a priority for the new nation. It took three years before Congress passed the Coinage Act of 1792, specifying the denomination and composition of the national money.

The ten coins were: the copper half cent ($0.005), the copper one cent ($0.01), the silver half "disme" ($0.05), the silver disme ($0.10), the silver quarter ($0.25), the silver half dollar ($0.50), the silver dollar ($1), the gold quarter eagle ($2.50), the gold half eagle ($5), and the gold eagle ($10). Curiously, even though the coin act called for its production, the copper coins were not legal tender, which meant they could be refused by banks. They did not become legal tender until 1850.

So the nation's first money system was, in theory, officially bimetallic—gold and silver, but it took even longer to bring all the coins into production. It wasn't until 1796 that production of gold coins even began. Although all these coins were legal tender, there were never enough produced to make them the exclusive currency of the nation. For instance, no gold quarter eagles were even minted between 1808 and 1821. Plus, the state-chartered, private banks were printing their own money, the value of which was always suspect, at best. So, people could not and did not rely solely upon the government's newly coined money.

The First National Bank

Another reason minting coins wasn't a political priority was because, during the same time period, Hamilton and the other Federalists pushed and succeeded at convincing

Congress to charter The First National Bank of the United States in 1791, which was everything that Hamilton and Morris hoped the defunct Bank of North America would be and more. The bank was private and controlled by private investors, but it was the official depository of all of the nation's money —a *central bank*.

The front story was that the national bank was needed to regulate all the state-chartered banks and to stabilize the currency. That sounded like a pretty good reason because although those banks were state-chartered, they weren't state-regulated. In fact, nobody was really regulating them. The banks were loaning and printing money based on the gold and silver coins in their vaults, much like the goldsmiths in Europe. However, the banks practiced a slightly different method of banking called *fractional reserve lending* while what the goldsmiths did could be called *whole reserve lending*. While the goldsmiths only printed promissory notes based on the gold they actually had, fractional reserve bankers could actually loan and print money with only a fraction of the gold or silver they had on hand. Put another way, they could lend more money than they actually had in their vaults.

If that sounds fishy, then it might be surprising to know is that is exactly how modern banking works in the United States and around the world. People who write checks for more money they have in their accounts in the hope they get paid before the checks are cashed are accused of 'kiting' checks because if all the checks are cashed at the same time, they bounce. This is called fraud, but banks do the same thing with loans all the time. They loan out the money that is deposited by customers, relying on the fact that all the customers don't come back at the same time to demand their money. *Most* of the time, it works. When it doesn't, it's called a 'run' on the bank and the bank goes out of business in a single day.

CHAPTER SEVEN: THE BANK

This happened all the time in early America. Even with fractional reserve lending, there are supposed to be *some* reserves in the vault – at least 10 percent. So, if $10,000 worth of loans were made, then there should have been at least $1,000 in the vault. However, with no one regulating them, many of these banks made loans and printed money with absolutely no coins in the vault. The addition of all this money based on nothing leads to *inflation*, an overabundance of money in circulation. The result was (and still is) each piece of money becomes worth *less* until the point it becomes completely *worthless*. And people who work real hours providing real goods and services end up with nothing for their trouble.

Clearly, the state-chartered private banks really did need regulating, but that's not what happened. The First National Bank was not a regulatory agency nor was its successor, the Second National Bank. They couldn't even regulate themselves. Huge scandals corrupted these national banks the same way the state banks were corrupted. Plus both the national banks printed their own paper money, but this was not the exclusive currency of the land. Every state-chartered bank also printed money.

One Nation under Many Currencies

So even with the nation firmly established under the Constitution, the nation's money supply was still a hodge-podge of literally hundreds of different kinds of money by 1811, the first year of the First National Bank. There were literally hundreds of state-chartered banks and one national bank issuing millions of US dollars in currency of questionable value and a government mint stamping out copper, silver, and gold coins in limited amounts. Plus, some foreign coins, such as the previously mentioned Spanish Real, were also legal tender. The Second National Bank would exit the scene by 1836, leaving the unreliable state banks in charge clear up until the Civil War.

Ten years after the scandals of the national banks, Congress managed to pass the legislation setting up the Independent Treasury system. This was the first and only time the national government attempted to completely divorce itself financially from the banking system.

Located in major cities around the nation, the Independent Treasury branches collected payments for tariffs, land sales, and other federal debts. The key was that they only accepted gold, silver, or federal Treasury notes as payment. State banks were not allowed to pay federal debts with their own bank notes; they had to pay with the coins in their vaults.

The effect was to put the nation on a gold/silver standard, reducing the reserves of state banks, which reduced, theoretically, the amount of money those banks could loan. The result was that for the first time, the federal government exerted some control over the nation's money supply.

Of course, that control was far from complete. Those state-chartered banks were slowed down a bit by the new federal requirements, but they continued to behave as they always had. The problem became so bad that these banks became known as 'wildcat' banks. A catalog had to be printed illustrating which US bank notes were good and which were bad. This went on up until the Civil War.

In the meantime, the Independent Treasury system faced other challenges as it attempted to present to the outside world a 'serious national currency' backed by gold and silver reserves.

CHAPTER SEVEN: THE BANK

The Shortcomings of the Gold Standard

At this point, it's really easy to get caught up in all the numerical details of how much gold or silver is worth in paper money and how those values change from nation to nation and from era to era. One key to understanding the gold vs. paper money debate is in understanding why nations want a currency backed by a precious metal or metals. First and foremost, it's about control of inflation. Printing money backed by a currency means a currency cannot be inflated beyond the amount of the gold and silver held by the bank. In theory, that's true, but it's not completely foolproof, as will be made evident shortly.

The other key is observing the overall history of the gold standard and finding the dominant trend, namely, that no country has ever succeeded at staying on a metallic standard through a major crisis which, nine times out of ten, is a major war. The reason is that a precious metals-backed currency cannot expand rapidly enough to handle the instant exponential increase in across-the-board spending waging war requires.

The Mexican American War of 1846 is the only major war in the history of the United States through which the government was able to remain on its bimetallic gold/silver standard and finance without borrowing from any bank.

However, the moment the US placed itself on the bimetallic standard with the implementation of the Independent Treasury system: it constantly struggled to remain on it until it was completely derailed by the Civil War. The main struggle with a precious metal-backed currency is keeping enough gold or silver in the vaults. In a closed system without trade with foreign governments, it would be relatively easy. Gold or silver going out would come back when the recipient spends the money, but in a system involving many nations, that gold or silver does not automatically come back. It can, and often does, end up in the vaults of multiple nations or other overseas banks.

The result for the US was that as the result of trade, gold steadily left the vaults of the Independent Treasury branches. Gold discovered during the California Gold Rush of 1849 offset some of these losses, but it was not enough. By 1853, the silver content of coins also had to be reduced. By 1857, the competition of foreign coinage had to be eliminated and the Spanish Real and all the other foreign coins that had been used as legal tender since before the American Revolution finally lost their legal tender status.

Civil War Bank Reforms Mandate

When the shots were fired at Fort Sumter in April 1861, the coin reserves had been reduced to almost nothing. Before the end of the year, the United States borrowed almost $200 million to take on the Confederacy. That same year, the US took itself off the gold and silver standard when it suspended payments of gold and silver to bearers of Federal Treasury notes. Although the Independent Treasury system hung on until 1921, eight years past the enactment of the Federal Reserve System in 1913, its real independence ended when the government's bank borrowing began for the Civil War.

And that was only the beginning. Legislation passed during the Civil War defines much of our currency and banking until this very day. The initial borrowing for the war still wasn't enough and the Lincoln administration took additional measures to increase the nation's money supply. The Treasury was authorized to print $50 million in promissory notes, which were used to pay the defense contractors and the salaries of soldiers.

However, these quickly began to depreciate in value, so the first version of the dollars Americans know and love came into being. The First Legal Tender Act of 1862 created the 'greenback,' because it was black on the front and green on the back, just as it is today. There were just two main differences. They were bigger than our current money, which changed in 1929 when they were reduced in size. The other difference was that these were emblazoned with the words 'United States Note,' rather than 'Federal Reserve Note,' which changed in 1913 with the founding of the Federal Reserve.

After setting up the greenback, the Lincoln administration went after the state banks with the goal of eliminating the legal tender they printed and increasing national control over the monetary supply. The National Banking Acts of 1863 and 1864 gave the federal government the power to charter national banks and created the office of Comptroller of the Treasurer to regulate those banks. Even though opponents argued that the chartering of banks and corporations was clearly a Constitutional power belonging to the states, the Supreme Court upheld the right of Congress to charter banks.

The initial precedent was McCulloch vs. Maryland of 1819, which upheld the Second National Bank because it was an 'implied power' of the federal government. What most people don't know is that besides the Supreme Court misspelling McCulloch's name (it's McColloh), Supreme Court Chief Justice John Marshall owned shares in the bank – not exactly an unbiased judge.

With the Constitutional challenges behind it, the National Banking Acts immediately chartered several national banks and re-chartered approximately 1,500 state banks nationwide as national banks. Regulation was now firmly in the hands of the federal government; all that was left were the state bank currencies floating around. A 10 percent tax levied on those bank notes inMarch1865 finally drove all the state bills from circulation.

One Currency Backed By Gold Or Silver—Who Cares?

For the first time in the history of the United States, there was one set of paper money and one set of coin money, but the debate about the gold standard versus fiat currency was far from over. Economists such as Henry Charles Carey argued for keeping the fiat-based currency, but the overall sentiment of the Congress and the White House was to return to the gold standard. From a wartime high of about $440 million, greenbacks were destroyed at a rate of $4 million a month. The destruction/reduction was halted at $347 million by 1878 because it triggered a depression; it remained at that level for more than one hundred years. Legislation passed in 1879 once again requiring the government to redeem paper dollars for gold.

After that, the nation spent the next twenty-one years being pulled back and forth by its bimetallic standard. It was gold versus silver. Some might ask why this debate even mattered. It boils down to economics and inflation, which we are told is bad. Yet inflation actually benefits those who borrow money – poor people – because as the currency inflates, causing each dollar to lose value, borrowers can pay back a loan with dollars that are worth less than the original dollars they borrowed. So, from a borrower's standpoint, the ideal currency is actually a fiat currency, but an unregulated currency benefits no one. The next best thing is a currency such as silver, which is more inflationary than gold. Thus it became the favored currency of the workingman.

Those who have a lot of money, or those who are owed a lot of money, want to maintain the value of that money to the greatest degree possible by having a currency that is the most deflationary. They wanted gold because it was 'sound money.' In 1900, the 'goldbugs,' as they were called, won the debate when the United States officially went on the Gold Standard. The dollar was set at $20.67 per troy ounce of gold. A troy ounce is slightly heavier than a standard ounce and has been the traditional measure of precious metals since the Middle Ages. Setting the dollar at $20.67 per troy ounce made the dollar literally redeemable for 1.5g of gold.

Adhering to a gold standard alone does not dictate a stable economy, which is evident given the bank panic of 2007 or the Great Depression decades earlier. However, such a standard does guarantee fiscal restraint as well as monetary stability and a suppression of inflation. In a gold standard economy, banks become more restricted in loaning money and leverage on loaning is suppressed and is usually are asset backed. Interest is new currency. This is why/how fractional reserve banking exists.

Congress Creates The Federal Reserve.

Congress succeeded in creating the Federal Reserve as a central bank. Comparisons have made of the Federal Reserve to the First and Second National banks, but it is somewhat different. The first two central banks were profit-maximizing commercial banks owned by private investors, with the government owning a minority stake. With a name like the Federal Reserve, it's easy to think the Federal Reserve is a government agency. Yet, it is no more a government agency than Federal Express. All nationally chartered banks are required to join and buy shares in the regional Federal Reserve banks. These shares cannot be sold or transferred and never earn more than a six percent return. Member banks also can vote on six of the nine members of the boards of their regional banks. These banks have six main duties: buy and sell U.S government securities on the open market; lend reserves to member banks; provide check-clearing services to all banks; issue new Federal Reserve Notes and collect the old ones; regulate the banks in their region to ensure they maintain their reserve requirements; and monitor banking and economic activity in their respective regions.

The government only has control over the seven-member Federal Reserve Board of Governors, which are appointed by the President and confirmed by Congress to serve 14-year terms. These governors along with the president of the New York Federal Reserve Bank and four rotating presidents from the other Federal Reserve banks comprise the Federal Open Market Committee (FMOC), which makes the major banking decisions in the country. The FMOC decides how much currency is printed and sets interest rates for the money of member banks.

Falling Off the Gold Standard—Twice

So with the Federal Reserve and the Gold Standard in place by 1913, no one would be faulted for believing that it would be smooth sailing for the economy from that point forward, but that was not the case. As stated before, adopting a gold standard is not as much of a problem as remaining on the gold standard. The Gold Standard held until the outbreak of World War I in Europe in 1914. American corporations had large European debts and their creditors came to collect in gold. Huge outflows of gold triggered the suspension of the Gold Standard and the closure of the New York Stock Exchange from July to December 1914.

Once again, paper fiat money was issued to stave off the crisis and the newly-established Federal Reserve set up a special fund to pay off the foreign creditors. All the other nations of the world abandoned the gold standard during the remainder of the war. As a neutral country from 1915 to 1917, the U.S was able to remain on the Gold Standard. Once the US joined the war, it modified the Gold Standard by banning the export of gold.

The wheels came off the Gold Standard by the time of the Great Depression. The British were the first to leave the gold standard in 1931 when depositors depleted gold reserves by demanding their money in gold. All the other countries of the world followed suit as depositors lost confidence in the banks. After a record number of bank failures in 1933, people lost confidence in paper currency and began to hoard gold. The Federal Reserves failed in its duties to shore up those banks or add money to the market to add liquidity to the market.

Roosevelt Bans Gold Ownership

Within his first week in office, President Franklin Roosevelt took the US off the Gold Standard, except for foreign transactions. He closed the banks to stop the runs on them, and signed Executive Order 6102 prohibiting anyone from possessing gold coins, gold bullion, and gold certificates within the continental United States. Those who couldn't move their gold had to surrender it to the government for $20.67 per troy ounce. Exemptions allowed owners to keep $100 in gold coins, historic coins, and gold used for artistic and industrial purposes. The order mainly affected the middle class because the rich had the means to move their gold reserves offshore and reap a substantial profit because once the government collected all the gold, it raised the price to $35 per troy ounce for international customers in 1934. This suddenly made the US Dollar an attractive investment and the United States ended up cornering the market on gold.

The US Dollar Becomes the World Standard

It also made the US currency the most stable in the world and all the major economies of the world were indirectly put on the Gold Standard as signatories to the 1944 Bretton Woods Agreements. Held in the closing days of World War II in the town of Bretton Woods in New Hampshire, the gathered nations agreed to peg their currency to the US Dollar as well as to the creation of the International Monetary Fund and the International Bank for Reconstruction and Development, which was later merged with the World Bank. The conference also established the rules for international banking, which became known as the Bretton Woods system.

The Gold Standard remained at $35 per troy ounce thereafter, but it never returned to the previous arrangement before the Great Depression. Instead, it became a Gold Exchange Standard under the Bretton Woods Agreements, allowing foreign dollar holders to exchange them for gold. The arrangement held up throughout the 1950s, butstarted to slowly unravel in the subsequent decades. The economy expanded rapidly in the 1960s and so did government spending.

President Lyndon Johnson succeeded in implementing his Great Society programs and signed off on a full-scale invasion of Vietnam. The result was that money flooded the system, causing inflation which lowered the value of the dollar and raised the price of gold. Johnson was urged to raise taxes to contract the money supply, but did not.

By 1968, it became impossible for the United States to keep the price of gold at $35 per troy ounce on the private market, so a two-tier system was developed. Central banks would trade gold at $35 per troy ounce, but the private gold market would be left to its own devices. Gold on the private market immediately jumped to $43 per troy ounce. It briefly settled back to $35 per troy ounce before starting to climb steadily from 1969 onwards.

The 'Shocking' End of the Gold Standard

From the 1960s into the 1970s, the economic pressures on the United States only increased; inflation caused the value of the paper dollar to plummet and gold continued to leave the country at an alarming rate. So on August 15, 1971, President Richard Nixon surprised the nation when he unilaterally ended the direct conversion of dollars into gold – the end of the Gold Standard. This became known as the Nixon Shock. With the currency no longer pegged to gold, the value of paper money fell and the value of gold rose to as much as $500 per troy ounce by 1980.

Instead of redeeming currency for gold, the banks of the world began holding US paper currency as the reserve currency in its vault. That is the cash redeemed for cash addressed earlier in the text for a fiat currency. Since 1971, the strength of the US dollar has been based on belief in the ability of the United States to pay its debts and/or borrow money. That belief has been shaken particularly hard since the financial crisis of 2008 and many nations are considering adopting a reserve currency other than the dollar.

THE PREMISE, THE MONEY & THE GOLD

Why Investors Need Non-Dollar Denominated Investments

During the mid-1970's, President Ford ended the ban on owning gold. People were allowed to invest in it as a commodity, which was particularly timely as inflation was out of control and gold is a good hedge against inflation, which causes dollar denominated investments to lose value. Bonds, life insurance policies, treasury certificates, and certificates of deposits are dollar denominated investments because they pay out in dollars. Those investments may earn positive interest, but if the dollars that make up the principal lose value, then the overall investment ends up being a loss. That's why investment counselors recommend a mix of dollar and non-dollar denominated investments such as gold because the government cannot print more of it.

The Gold Standard is gone and the Federal Reserve has been in charge since 1913, yet there have been two major Depressions, several recessions, and multiple banking bailouts during that time period. Proponents of the Federal Reserve System refer to the boom-bust cycle as the 'business cycle' and deem it an inevitable part of the modern economy. Conspiracy theorists believe the Federal Reserve manipulates the monetary supply to further its own ends.

Perhaps the truth lies somewhere in between. It could be strongly argued that the Federal Reserve could be eliminated if fractional reserve borrowing was eliminated because it automatically builds inflation into the system. For every dollar the Federal Reserve puts into the system, that same $1 becomes $10 in loans, creating huge bubbles. If the banks loaned dollar for dollar, it would curtail inflation, maintain the value of currency and ensure the growth that occurs is sound. So what is the average investor to do with all of this?

Do what George is preparing to do.

Chapter Eight
THE INFORMATION

CHAPTER EIGHT: THE INFORMATION

IN THE WORDS OF DAVID MONK, MONEY IS AN INTELLECTUAL SPORT; either you can play or you can't. The acquisition of financial resources to the point of never needing money again is a nuanced endeavor with mental land mines everywhere. It is extremely treacherous because knowing valuable information doesn't help you become wealthy – only using it can accomplish wealth.

This is why the road to wealth is littered with good intentions, academic degrees; lost opportunities and tons of excuses on every corner. Once you eliminate lottery winners, trust fund babies, executives who left companies with a $25 million parachute, and well-to-do divorcees, you are left with those who reached the top by thinking, and thinking properly.

Now, don't mistake thinking for an inactive activity; learning how to think properly is exhausting because there are so many wrong options you must first ignore. There's almost a secret code to proper thinking. And this code is hidden from the average person. You may have heard people say they built their business or wealth on hard work, and that is often the case. But the very fact they knew how to work and not just work for 'work's' sake means they were thinking correctly.

The very fact that someone starts a business says they have thought about this option and properly concluded that wealth, especially generational wealth, can only arise from ownership and/or control of a corporation. But there is another maturation point for the most influential, wealthiest families in history. Once they got the money, they wanted the gold. The currency of power is gold. There are no gold printing presses. For centuries, political, social, and religious forces have leveraged vested interests in keeping real money the exclusive property of those in control. You can have all the paper money you want; all the government wants is the gold. But again, how did the narrative get changed?

Misinformation is sadly the nut and bolt that keep the US economy tightly fastened. Misinformation can be warm and comforting, especially during times of economic upheaval. The masses have always preferred ignorance to knowledge. Few will admit it, but being lied to creates a weird internal satisfaction. For things to change, investors would have to recalibrate their current thinking processes. And the very fact few will admit this proves this point. But knowing, accepting and implementing the truth as it relates to your money is more than a notion.

To understand why accurate information is so rare, you must first understand this: accurate information is dangerous, dangerous to the person in possession of the information, and dangerous to the status quo in charge of keeping deception as sexy as possible. Accurate information throws off the balance of society; there's simply no room for it. So who has accurate investment information? The top one percent.

The top one percent of any society controls the wealth of that society. Smart people have always found even smarter people to advise them in regard to their assets and investments. The US government is the smartest financial advisor in the world, though you have to watch carefully to notice. This is because the government doesn't actually offer the advice to others; it takes its own advice and makes quiet moves in its own best interest.

The government invests, just like every other investor, and by doing so shows where its confidence is. If you follow the government's investing strategies, it may lead you in some very interesting – and unexpected – directions. First, you start with the largest treasury in the world. Second, you find that this treasury believes that gold has the best value in the world.

CHAPTER EIGHT: THE INFORMATION

The conclusion is obvious: the richest nation in the world puts most of its belief in the value of gold. The top one percent understands this dynamic. The general public does not.

Government and Wall Street thrive on misinformation. They hand it out on a daily basis to keep the masses comfortable and 'safe.' The government produces that fictional story called paper money. The public, as we've seen, believes this fiction, and treats paper money as a valuable product, the currency of the country.

But this phantom value called paper money isn't the only fiction the government peddles. Since the 70s, the government has been selling another fiction – that gold is worth less than it is, that the American economy is doing better than it is....

The government needs these fictions to be accepted as truth, because they solidify the country's position amongst its citizenry. If the public believes that the American economy will recover, they'll invest time and money in that belief, thereby helping the American economy rebound from its lows. If other countries believe the government's story that the economy is rebounding, they too will offer money as investment.

Beyond that, the psychological cost of telling the public the truth – about the economy, the dollar, even the gold in Fort Knox – would be mass chaos and panic. Can you imagine the reaction of the public if the government decided one day to tell them, "We may have exaggerated. There's only half as much gold as we told you and, on the international market the American dollar is worth 1/3 of what we told you." The public would panic, leading to runs on banks around the country. The rest of the world would panic, and hundreds of other countries would pull their money from American banks and begin demanding that the American government pay their debts – immediately. The American government – and country – would go bankrupt.

So the government sells fiction for the public as well as itself. Its purpose, at the core, is to self-preserve the selected distribution of wealth. In other words, the wealthy must remain that way – forever. The one percent of people who control the wealth of this country are the ones who know how to make the money in the first place. They understand the lunacy of fiat currency and the value of gold. In the act of making money, they've come to know the systems and fictions handed out by the government. They've even learned to utilize them. For the most part, they've also learned to keep their mouths shut. After all, they don't particularly want to share their wealth, and they certainly don't want to see the American government tumble from panic, so mums the word.

What else does the one percent know that the rest of us don't? Well, they know how to handle their money, to start with. They know when and where to invest, and what constitutes safety or risk. They know how to keep their money safe. The one percent understands the true value of gold. This, though, falls under the heading of things the public is not 'supposed' to know. If the public started investing in physical gold rather than stocks and bonds, Wall Street would crumble. Beyond that, the flow of money that supports the government and American dollar – through stock and bond investing – would cease. This alone would cause big problems for the American government. It would signify the end of one of their major income streams.

This, then, is why the American public isn't encouraged to participate in gold. The 'system' won't continue ticking unless the public's wealth is pumped back into the government via stock and bond investing.

CHAPTER EIGHT: THE INFORMATION

When an investor steps out of line and discusses placing his money in financial vehicles that aren't approved by the 'system,' all hell breaks loose. There are no provisions set aside for independent thinking, no contingency for knowledgeable investors. People like that just don't fit. Oh, the brokers don't mind if you read a few books and scan some Internet articles, as long as you keep your money in the brokerage firm, and ultimately invest in what they recommend.

In fact, the complaints heard by clients are used to point towards the perfect in-house product that ironically overcomes that exact objection. Investors who understand how the economy really works almost become whistle blowers, and whistle blowers cause lots of problems for themselves, as George is about to discover.

***

Arriving back in Austin from The Combine conference, George stopped to pick up a few things up from the grocery store before heading home. All he could think about is what he learned in New York. He was resolute now. Nothing would get in the way of making investments in gold. Carol planned a dinner with friends and family. It was going to be a big gathering and, in classic George style, he would control the conversation, telling everyone in the most loving way possible all they had missed.

George walked into the fresh market and was immediately recognized by his broker.

"George! How's it going?"

"Hey, Ernest, what perfect timing," George answered. Ernest was a bit confused by the "perfect timing" reference - but continued.

"Haven't seen you at the club lately; what's your handicap these days?"

"You haven't seen me because I'm no longer a member. Can't afford it. Remember that IPO you put me onto that was a 'sure bet?'"

"Oh, *that*. It sure did tank! Got a hell of commission out of it though," Ernest let slip of private egocentrism.

Pause.

"Are you listening?"

"Oh, yes, sure. I'm listening," replied Ernest.

"I couldn't even get a hold of you the day it happened. Guess you were too busy enjoying the commission."

Ernest hid his embarrassment behind a cup of coffee.

George coughed.

"I'm not a young man anymore. Can't go out and replace what you keep losing. My wife hasn't worked outside the home in years."

"No, sure, I understand," Ernest replied.

"That's why I want to divest 15 percent of my stocks and bonds and increase my holdings in gold accordingly."

"C'mon, George, we've got you invested in 5 percent of our precious metals fund already. And it's doing well and I . . ."

"I know you do, but I want to go to 20 percent and I want physical gold."

"Twenty percent?! Are you kidding me? And lose all that value tied up in your stocks?"

"What value? I'm down 50%.

"I know, but you've got to see the big picture and invest for the long haul."

"I don't have time to wait around for the long haul. I have to start thinking about the short haul, Ernest. What was it John Maynard Keynes said? 'In the long run, we are all dead.' Right now, I need to preserve what we have before there's nothing left."

CHAPTER EIGHT: THE INFORMATION

"You really should go home and think it over. Talk it over with the wife."

"I have, Ernest. She thinks we should put all of our money in gold. Build a great big vault in our basement and keep it there. I had to talk her out of all of that. I was lucky to get her to agree to 20 percent. She doesn't trust brokers."

"Oh, my."

"It's downright scary right now. The debt . . ."

George interrupted himself with another cough, this time holding his chest tightly.

"The debt crisis and the instability of the Euro. All that could come back to bite us."

"I couldn't agree more," Ernest responded. "That's why I want to keep you in stocks because stocks eventually work. In fact, even before you came in, I was going to schedule our annual portfolio review and talk to you about shifting the rest of your holdings out of bonds and into more equities."

"How can you ask me to do that? Haven't you heard a word I've been telling you? How can you stand there with a straight face and recommend stocks, as poorly as they have been performing?"

"Look, ride this out a little longer and you'll see the market recover. The Dow has climbed over the 12,000 mark and things are already beginning to pick up. If you pull out of the stocks and invest in precious metals, you're going to lose money and the chance to recover your former losses. Precious metals don't grow and if you invest in them at the level you're talking about, your portfolio is never going to grow. We've got you in our own precious metals in-house fund and it will do well for you."

"That's the other thing. I want to get out of that, too. You guys really don't get it – the whole point of owning precious metals. Or you don't want to get it, because there goes all your commissions. Right? Because once my money is in gold or silver, that's it. There's nothing more in it for you. But with stocks, you can move money around and collect a commission every time that you do. The whole point of investing in precious metals is to come away with something tangible, something in your hand. You know it's not going to be swallowed up when the stock market tanks; the investment is as "good as gold – because it is gold."

Ernest answered George with no consideration of what was just said, "Ok, I got it; we put you in a gold ETF, an Exchange Traded Fund. It's similar to a mutual fund, except shares of an ETF can be bought or sold throughout the day on an exchange, but only by an authorized broker/dealer such as myself."

"Ok, let me understand this. First, you can hear. Second, you heard me and third, your response is to put me in virtual gold? A bunch of electronic blips on a screen?"

"C'mon George. I know some of the investments I had you in before didn't work out. If it makes you feel any better, a lot of them didn't work out for me, either," Ernest replied.

"Comforting."

"An economic storm is coming," George said. "Investment needs to take tangible form these days. Gold is the answer. Remember the banking system *shut down* in 2008. The only thing that averted financial catastrophe was a giant bailout from the taxpayers, but the underlying problems are still there. Nothing but watered-down reforms have been put into place, so everything is still on course for another meltdown. And the next time, we won't be able to afford another bailout because the country is mortgaged up to its eyeballs. The nation's debt is now 103 percent of GDP. Do you know what that means?"

"Yes, I know what it means," Ernest answered reluctantly.

CHAPTER EIGHT: THE INFORMATION

"It means that if you took all the wealth of the country generated in a year, including every scrap of food from the mouths of every man, woman, and child, it would still would not be enough to pay off all of the nation's debts. The GDP for the United States was $14.59 trillion in 2010 – the last year of available figures – while our national debt is $15.7 trillion and continues to rise. We're borrowing money from China – a country that we once regarded as an enemy and never as an ally since they became Communist – to finance our debt. Now there's talk of using another currency besides the dollar as the world's reserve currency. You know, these are the dollars other nations have kept in their vaults since the end of World War II to back up their own currencies," George said.

"I know, I know."

"Some said the Euro might be the world's new reserve currency, but look at all the troubles it's having, with the debt crisis in Greece, France, Italy, Spain, Portugal, and I won't even get into the problems in Eastern Europe. Countries that once would have never considered leaving the Euro are discussing their options."

George grabbed his chest and coughed deeper and harder.

"Need water?" Ernest asked.

"I'm ok."

"Look, your earlier point is right," Ernest conceded.

"So that leaves the Chinese Yuan and all the talk of the 21st century being the Chinese Century, just like the 20th Century was the American Century. I've heard all that before. Remember when Japan was supposed to surpass America and the world? It seemed like they were buying up all of America. And then the banks tightened up the money supply and left the Japanese holding the bag. The banks called in the loans, just like they did for the stock traders of 1929, and the mortgage lenders of 2008, forcing a mass sell-off of real estate. That in turn flooded the market, making each subsequent sale worth less than the previous one. The result was a ten-year recession in Japan and the end of talk about Japanese dominance."

"You're right; people quit talking about Japan. I never really noticed it. Where did you get all this information from anyway?" Ernest asked.

"David Monk."

"David who?

"Monk - like the robes."

"Oh, I've never…"

"You wouldn't have; he's not one of you. Anyway, most people don't connect the dots. And the same thing is going to happen with China because they are up to their armpits in American debt. Factories are already being idled over there because consumer spending has declined here. Making the Yuan the world's reserve currency is like a dry-rotted floor that will fail if the US should default. And that was something that nobody ever talked about until now. It's because of all these things that I want my money in gold and precious metals."

"Okay, we'll liquidate your stocks and invest them in our precious metals fund."

"No, Ernest. Liquidate that, too, and get me invested in physical metals. I want to hold real bars of gold and silver ASAP."

"I don't think that's a good idea."

"That's actually a great indicator because your ideas have made me lose my club membership and by the way, whose money is this anyway? It's my money. You're my broker. You work for me. When I say I want out, I want out."

"Okay, it's done. I'll get the paperwork started."

"Once that's done, we'll see where I want to go from there. It may end up that 20 percent precious metals might be

CHAPTER EIGHT: THE INFORMATION

a low number. Depending on what happens, I may want to get out of the market altogether."

***

What Your Stock Broker Can't Tell You

There exists a disconnection between popular understanding of stock brokers, and a broker's true function. A benefit of the market turmoil is that investors begin to revisit long-held assumptions about Wall Street, stock brokers and diversification.

One long-held assumption has been that stock brokers have their client's best interests as priority one. Another is that a stock broker truly understands portfolio management, diversification and alternative investing. Such assumptions are terribly incorrect.

This may come as a surprise, but your stock broker is not there to make you money. He is there to make money from you. Nowhere in a broker's job description is there any mention of making money for the client. Their job is to generate commissions. Consequently, other investments that may be more appropriate for your portfolio are not offered if these investments do not directly benefit the broker, and the brokerage house. This cannot be overstated.

Your stock broker's business is buying and selling securities. If your portfolio grows in the process, so-be-it. The objective, however, is to make money from your account. Period.

The Brokerage Firm
A stock broker is called a 'broker' because he facilitates the objectives of the buyer and seller as a middle person. Say for instance, you desire to buy 100 shares of a stock. You call your broker and place a 'buy market' order. Your broker then goes into the open market electronically and purchases the shares on your behalf. This, on the surface, seems to be a very simple, straightforward transaction. The broker makes his money from commissions earned from your account. Various firms charge various amounts on a 'per share' or 'per transaction' basis. Either way, your 'buy order' generates money for the stock broker. This in and of itself is still not necessarily a problem.

Conflict surfaces when investment choices presented to clients are defined by those transactions that provide greatest commissions to the broker. This naturally limits your options. Retail brokers, by law, cannot offer private equity investments, such as privately held commercial property to the general, non-accredited public. Limited investment choices can substantially elevate portfolio risk during volatile markets.

Alternative Investments
Alternative investments are just that - alternatives. These investment choices are not found in the traditional capital markets. However, alternative investments can be invaluable for hedging traditional holdings. The portfolio that holds stocks and bonds exclusively, no matter how well diversified, has unnecessary exposure to the unpredictability of market forces.

The expansion of one's investment portfolio to include private equity holdings can provide another layer of

CHAPTER EIGHT: THE INFORMATION

stabilized yields. Although there are licensing requirements stock brokers must meet, their sophistication as it relates to alternative investing is extremely limited. It is up to the individual investor to seek prudent guidance as to the most appropriate alternative investments for his or her portfolio. It isn't too late. A clear understanding of what your stock broker can and cannot provide is the beginning of more profitable investing.

Dinner

George arrived home. The dinner table was loud and joyous. George told story after story of his time in New York. Carol had made his favorite, which was turkey in any form.

George couldn't stop coughing, hard and dry.

Carol heard him but didn't show her concern. George pressed his napkin hard over his mouth to muffle the sound. In the napkin was blood, but he didn't notice; the cranberry sauce hid it perfectly.

"The investment combine was unbelievable." George said.

"I personally witnessed millions of dollars being saved in real-time," he told family and friends. "The information was scary, literally, like a horror flick."

"Dad, stop exaggerating," his son, Shawn, begged from the other end of the table.

"Well, losing money is scary, son," George said. "Imagine how scary it would be if you didn't have any food to feed your face."

The entire table burst into snickers at the sixteen-year old who was six-feet two, one hundred ninety pounds and growing like weeds. Shawn took over the table conversation, recalling his dad's obsession with saving and investing money.

"Ok, let's look around; my dad is so frugal, so detailed with his money, he has made us all come to his house to hear him talk about it, as if we didn't know."

The table laughed.

"Dad, remember when you made me go back into Wal-Mart because the sign said 20% off but you figured out they'd only given up 19.9%; do you remember that? We stood at customer service for thirty minutes trying to figure out how they could give us one-tenth of a penny."

The melody of tingling knives and forks filled the air as story after story circulated around the table.

While in New York, George and David Monk had an opportunity to speak in more detail than was possible from the stage. In fact, George had all but hired David Monk's firm to manage his money, at least as much of it was left after the market downturn. As soon as his positions were liquidated, he was moving his business. Three days after arriving back in Austin and instructing his broker to sell, George contacted Monk's office, arranged a meeting and traveled to Ft. Lauderdale, Florida to personally sit with Monk. This would change everything.

***

Rob, Monk's irreplaceable assistant, led George past the front desk and down a long hallway that intertwined in and out of doors requiring credentials. George entered the waiting room that led to Monk's abode and through its door, he saw her sitting there. Danielle.

He'd heard so much. In arranging this meeting with Monk, Robbie had provided George with a detailed overview of Monk's organizational style, and critical information on

CHAPTER EIGHT: THE INFORMATION

what made Monk tick. Sitting there in the waiting room, George understood why Robbie only refers to Danielle as 'The Queen.'

He could see her sitting on a white leather couch directly under a rich, impeccably executed oil painting. Depicted was a country-side sunset against a bluish purple sky. Yet it was she, Danielle, who was the flawless portrait of pure beauty. George struggled not to stare; she smiled and eased his anxiety.

Danielle played an irreducible role in David Monk's life – a woman of few words who wields limitless influence. She's as insightful as David is smart. They are the perfect couple with complimentary talents. She, a woman of Cuban heritage who doesn't speak Spanish, presents as a California liberal but possesses conservative politics. Their connection was immediate, stronger than anything either had experienced before. Although first drawn to her long flowing dark hair, and a body sculptured by the gods, it was her care and concern for Monk's personal success that 'sealed the deal.' And this care had allowed Monk to lay down many demons at her feet; his many unhealthy vices now gone.

David spotted George and walked out of his office to greet him.

"George!"

"David, how are you?"

"Great," Monk answered. "Meet Danielle."

Danielle nodded and gracefully left the room.

"They really like you here," George said to Monk.

"They like money."

Monk concentrated on answering another question not asked.

"So what do I think of paper money? I think it's the

143

greatest scam imposed on humanity. That said, we all need it. A terrible irony, huh?"

The two sat in Monk's office and, over the next two hours, Monk explained in greater detail the solution for George's investments moving forward. But it wasn't until George asked one question did you gain insight as to why Monk was so passionate about gold.

"Why do you love gold so much?" he asked.

Monk smiled differently this time. The gut emotion didn't seem to be based solely on market data. Monk leaned forward and told George his story.

"It was 2 a.m. and unusual in that I wasn't asleep," Monk said. "Maybe it was celebratory debris still in the air from a day of birthday events. To finally be 10 years old was monumental; things would probably change now, at least I thought they should. More responsibility, fewer rules, and yes, more allowance. The type of allowance that would upgrade my hobby set to one more representative of a kid on the move. I thought I'd begin the first day of my second decade by separating my gold coins from my other money so I wouldn't spend it. I looked all around the hotel room for a safe place to keep the 10 coins my aunt sent for my birthday. We'd be looking for another room the next day so I just needed a place for the night away from my brother and sister's view. I found the golden location. Behind the water faucets at the bottom rear of the toilet, no one could see it. I carefully stacked my gold coins there. The coins were hidden so well I thought I might forget them; maybe that's why I was still up, staring into the darkness. Surely I wouldn't leave in the morning and forget to crawl down there and retrieve them. Just when my thoughts were finally turning towards sleep, a figure moved in the room. At first, I wasn't sure whether it was my brother

CHAPTER EIGHT: THE INFORMATION

or sister getting up for a restroom trip, but something deep inside told me not to make a sound.

In an effort not to make a noise, I kept my head still and starting watching only with the east to west movement of my eyes. I watched as the figure started to emerge out of the darkness of the unlit room. My eyes had been open for a while and had taken hold of the moonlight. 'Oh, my God!' I thought, 'A man is in our hotel room.' He slowly moved from one piece of luggage to the next, then to my mothers' purse removing her wallet, food stamps and identification. By this time, fear had set in so firmly that I was unsure whether I could actually move if I wanted to. My body felt heavier than ever, like I was in a strait-jacket with an anchor on my chest.

The man – by this time, I was sure it was a man – proceeded to rummage through my knit coin sack; my mother had made one for all the kids. He pulled out the few dollars we had in the world. It ran through my mind how this burglar must not know that was all the money we had to eat on cause you're not supposed to steal from poor people.

My fear partnered with frustration, and then anger as my ten-year-old mind attempted to process how my mom would feel once she found out we had been robbed. Lost on me was the tangible danger my family was actually in. I knew not if his plan was to kill all six of us, or harm us physically in any way.

I did know that as quickly as he had appeared, he was gone and I would have credited my memory to a nightmare had it not been for the police sirens that stirred me awake the next morning. I got up repeatedly asking, 'Mom, what happened?' Her only reply, 'We've been robbed.' She then turned back to the police officer and continued speaking.

As if flashcards were thrust in my face, I immediately recalled everything that happened the night before. With a shaking voice and sweaty hands, I shouted with my eyes shut tight. 'I saw the Man!' The policeman stopped writing.

Mom turned sharply with a look of disbelief and horror and slowly asked me, 'You saw him?'

'Yes,' I replied. 'I was up late because I couldn't sleep and I saw this man walking in the room.' I continued, 'I didn't want to wake anybody because I was scared to death. I wasn't sure what he would do.' I went on to explain how he went through my mothers' purse, took her wallet, identification and everything else she had and then left as quickly as he came . . .

I heard my mother murmur under her voice. 'He took everything, officer; he took all the money we had.'

I paused, pulled on her elbow and said, 'Wait, I hid my gold.' I will never forget how that man took our money, but he didn't take our gold, and it was those few coins that fed us until we could get into another shelter. As long as you have gold, you can survive."

George nodded and suddenly realized he had barely been breathing the entire time. He made up his mind at that moment that as soon as he returned home, he would transfer $800,000 to Monk's firm. He would finally follow his gut – but there was something else he needed to deal with.

Chapter Nine
THE CONFRONTATION

CHAPTER NINE: THE CONFRONTATION

THE RELATIONSHIP STARTED OUT INNOCENTLY – all dangerous things do; small courtesies in the office over time became small birthday cards, becoming larger birthday cards, quick lunches, longer dinners and eventually overnights while George was on the road.

On the Monday before Stanley's Tuesday doctor's visit to receive his biopsy results, Gozi and George had a rather intense argument based on his empty promise to leave Carol, his wife. The unethical nature of their relationship became irrelevant as larger unethical behaviors came into play, namely, sex.

Until now, Gozi's reputation as a complete professional had been unsullied. She had been Dr. Angelo's right hand twenty years. Patients asked their opinions of Dr. Angelo's practice faithfully credited the 'patient care' portion to Gozi. She had the caring approach, she had the thoroughness of detail, and she had an inappropriate relationship with George.

If you knew what to look for, there were small indicators of her non-medical related dealings with George in his chart. Each time he would come and visit, a smiley face was placed at the end of the notes for that day. Small, unnoticeable emotional marking that would never be connected. That dinner, on that Monday evening would prove fatal.

"So why are you still with her?"

"That's an unanswerable question," George responded.

"For you, all questions are," Gozi answered. "That is your way of keeping me at bay. I've all but accepted another position in an effort to spend my entire life with you."

"Gozi, we've had this conversation."

"True, but you know what? This isn't going to end like this."

"What does that mean?" George asked.

"It means you fucked my life over and me in the process. I'm your toilet."

The approaching waiter didn't discern the bad timing.

"Sir, another glass of wine?"

George waved his hands, quickly sending him on his way.

"You can't be serious."

"This was a mutual arrangement."

"An arrangement? What am I, a floral bouquet?" Gozi began to become noticeably irate.

"So here's the summary, George. You like summaries. You and I have been sleeping together five years now. I've traveled all over the country so you could have your happy meal waiting for you in your room. Why do you think I did this? It was because I actually started to believe we were going to be together."

"Baby," George tried to calm her down.

"What an asshole," she responded and then continued in an intense whisper that seemed to get louder by the second.

"Do you realize the shit hole I would be in if Dr. Angelo ever got a hint of our relationship? Do you know I wouldn't be able to work another day in this town if all this came to light? For you, I risked throwing everything away. For you – of all people."

"I always said this would be a risk on both of our parts. I have a wife, a kid heading to college, and a mother who lives with me. Stakes are high on this end, but I thought you and I had something that was worth the risk."

"Me too, and based on that premise, I made decisions that are now coming back to haunt me. You aren't leaving Carol, are you?"

CHAPTER NINE: THE CONFRONTATION

George paused and motioned for the waiter to bring more wine. He thought for a moment, "I am not."

Gozi sat back in her chair, and with both hands, shoved her hair behind her ears.

"You got me, you really got me."

"We can still spend time together; nothing has to change. I am in this for the long haul," George insisted.

"For the long haul? The long haul? There is no long haul," Gozi said.

"You want a vagina, not a relationship. I was the fool to think otherwise. Through all of those tests and the late nights I took your file home and explained things you needed to know. The times I referred you to additional doctors you wouldn't have known about had I not taken an interest in you as my future husband. You got me," Gozi said.

George pulled his chair closer to the table. He reached for her hand. She pulled it from under his.

"At the very beginning of this, I said you would have to be patient, that all of this would take time to unravel if indeed it ever unraveled. But seeing Shawn grow up, and the responsibilities of keeping mom, the sacrifices Carol has made to keep the home halfway decent has caused me to reconsider. It's caused me to reconsider whether what we're doing is good."

"It's never been good, but it was good enough to keep you doing it, I guess," Gozi said.

George tried to continue talking, but Gozi interrupted.

"I tell you what – let's make this a clean break starting now. Listen to what I'm about to say, George. Never call, don't send gifts and don't ever fix your mouth to ask me to travel with you again. I'm done."

Gozi got up, put on her handmade jacket which was a Valentine's gift from George the year before. She paused.

"Thank you, George, for destroying my life." She slipped her purse off the arm of the chair and walked away.

***

The water in the tub was running ten minutes after Gozi walked into her well-decorated condominium. The familiar beige chart was sitting on the kitchen counter, "Stanley, George" on its protruding lip. She'd taken his chart home the Friday before to discuss some results with him over the weekend, just as they'd done many times before while sitting on her couch in the heat of summer and cold of holidays. George always seemed to make time for her.

"*Gotta get this back into the office,*" she thought. But there were a few things that needed erasing since she would probably never take his file home again. She flipped through the weeks and months of his records and saw the tiny smiley faces. There were also small stars, underlined words with no relationship to his medical condition such as "anatomy," and "lower back," which had become their code words for sex. She was off on Tuesday, but would return the file first thing Wednesday morning as she always opened the office and spent the first thirty minutes there alone. In medical files, the first name of the patient is written last. Only once before in her twenty years of health care experience had she come across two individuals with names similar enough to cause any real problems - until now. Her lover, George Stanley, shared the exact same name in reverse order as another one of Dr. Angelo's patients, Stanley George. There were other odd similarities; both men were the same age and shared conditions in their chest; other than that, there were enough

CHAPTER NINE: THE CONFRONTATION

differences to prevent the medical staff from ever making a mistake in identity.

***

On Tuesday morning, Stanley George walked into Dr. Angelo's office to receive his biopsy results. Dr. Angelo asked Betty, a new hire brought in to assist Gozi, to hand her the chart. She gave the doctor the only chart there. It read, "George, Stanley."

Dr. Angelo looked down briefly at Stanley's chart, which in reality wasn't his, gave him the wrong diagnosis and basically asked him to prepare to die. Based on the logical premise that Dr. Angelo had the right chart in her hand, that the results were accurate and that there were no other options possible especially because a respected, seasoned physician said there weren't, Stanley had engaged on a psychological path that wasn't his own. His bad premise caused him to borrow pain. Bad premise makes you relax when you should be paranoid. In this case, bad premise fooled the physician and the patient. Time, chance and Murphy's Law did the rest. Bad premise creates virtual realities that have tangible, real world consequences.

It was early Wednesday morning, 7:30 am; George's son, Shawn, had just completed his two mile run and was standing in the front yard tossing a football to himself. George, who would himself be leaving for work in an hour, saw Shawn from the living room window and decided to walk outside.

"Throw!" George said motioning with his hands wide.

"Oh boy - Dad, don't hurt yourself."

"You're funny. Throw the ball," George replied.

Carol was upstairs preparing to shower when she

heard conversation through the window above the front lawn. She moved to get a peek. George was back-peddling to catch a ball already in flight. She smiled. George wound up and threw the ball back to Shawn in a straight arrow.

He bent over and coughed.

"We need to go back to the doctor, he's coughing too frequently," Carol thought to herself. She turned the knob and started the hot water. As steam began to fill the bathroom, she turned on her radio to listen to the oldies but goodies broadcast. She never missed one – it was the soundtrack to her morning. As soon as she hit the power button, that song began to play, the one that always her tears her up. Sinatra.

"And now the end is near, and so I face the final curtain. My friend, I'll make it clear, I'll state my case of which I'm certain. I've lived a life that's full, traveled each and every highway, and more - more than this, I did it my way. Regrets – I've had a few..."

"Riiiing! The phone.

Jarred out of the moment, Carol slipped on her robe and ran to the night stand in the bedroom.

"Who could this be?" she thought before touching the receiver.

"Hello?"

"Is this Mrs. Stanley?" The voice said on the other end.

"It is."

The other end went silent for a split second longer than comfortable. The kind of split second that bothers you, but you don't know why.

"Hi, this is Gozi at Dr. Angelo's office. The doctor would like to see George as soon as possible. We can schedule an appointment for this afternoon if that works with your schedule." Gozi said.

CHAPTER NINE: THE CONFRONTATION

"Well yes - that should be no problem. Uhh - is there a problem?" Carol asked.

"Doctor would like to go over his test results.'

"But we already went over the results. Has something new come up?"

"Doctor can explain everything in more detail than I can."

"Ok, I'll make sure we get to the office this afternoon."

"Thank you, Mrs. Stanley," Gozi said.

"No, thank you," Carol responded.

"Oh, and tell George hello," Gozi hung up.

Carol stepped back into the bathroom now thick with steam, mint and pomegranate smells in the air. She turned her radio back up and began singing with Sinatra while looking back out the window to the front lawn.

"...I've loved, laughed and cried, I've had my fill – my share of losing, but now as tears subside - I find it all so amusing. To think I did all that and may I say not in a shy way. No, no, not me; I did it my way."

George was still playing with Shawn, his briefcase discarded on the brick walkway leading to the house, his keys laying in the tall grass.

"*He's gonna be sweaty before work,*" Carol thought. She wondered whether to call down and interrupt his morning father- son pickup game or just let him come back inside first. He always came in and said goodbye, and gave her a kiss before leaving. She stepped into the shower, having yet to tell George they needed to go to the doctor. In between lathers, her mind couldn't help but wonder what the call was all about, and that maybe it had something to do with his terrible cough. Possibly he was under- medicated and needed larger doses. Whatever it was, they would find out.

"Tell George I said hello?" Carol repeated the last thing Gozi said. "Interesting."

"Ok, one more, son!" George shouted to Shawn from across the front yard. It was getting late and time to head into the office. Shawn tossed the ball in perfect arc, and George caught it with collegiate-like form.

"Ooooh – not bad for an old man," Shawn commented.

"Old man?" George snapped back. "When I was in the ninth grade, I had the fastest 40 yard sprint time in the entire school."

Shawn rolled his eyes as he'd heard this story one time less than one million. George picked up the ball and jogged over to Shawn to begin another story.

"And then when I got to college I had recruits all over me, because I was a multi-athlete."

"A multi-athlete, dad?" Shawn said. "Is that even a word?"

"Bottom line is I could play any sport; I just had the talent." George said as he tucked his shirt back into his pants and looked around for his keys.

Carol was humming another soft tune. She turned up the radio to accompany her as she got louder. This was her most peaceful moment of each day before she had to take care of her mother-in-law and start thinking about the list of things not finished from the day before.

She sat down on the shower stool, allowing the hot water to run through her hair. George would be up any moment now.

"Alright, triathlete," Shawn said. "At least you can still catch a ball or two so that gives me hope that I'll be able to play for a while myself."

George coughed, put his hand on his son's shoulder and pulled him close.

CHAPTER NINE: THE CONFRONTATION

"Son, I'm proud of you."

"Thanks, dad. I've never heard you say that."

"I know, and that's going to change. We're going to spend more time together. It's just time to do that; in fact, we're way overdue."

The two embraced and Shawn headed for the front door as George remotely unlocked his car and threw his briefcase in the backseat.

"Is that you, honey!" Carol turned down the radio and shouted downstairs. She thought she heard the door chime.

"It's me, mom!" Shawn shouted back.

"Ok!" Carol turned her favorite show radio back up. Shawn walked into the kitchen to finish the half-eaten bagel he'd started before his morning run. He flipped on the television and sat on the couch to catch a little morning entertainment before launching his day. After a few minutes, he lowered the volume of Good Morning America. He almost could hear something, but not really.

"What's that noise?" he thought.

Slowly, he got up and walked back into the living room. It was a low rumble, an idle.

Shawn opened the front door. His dad's car door was still open.

"Dad, you still here?'

He moved from behind the bush obstructing his view.

George was slumped over the wheel.

"What?"

Shawn raced out the door screaming.

"Dad!"

His father's position told him something was very wrong, very critical, very out of place. One leg was outside the car door, barely touching the ground. The other bent upwards.

The car was still in park, the news radio still on with the day's weather reports playing in the background.

He picked up his father, pulled him out of the front seat and laid him on the ground. He screamed like only a son can.

"Ma, call 911!"

"What was that?" Carol whispered to herself. The water was running over her ears and something seemed to pierce the atmosphere - but she couldn't quite make it out. *"Probably Shawn coming in and out,"* she thought.

Shawn bent over his father checking for vital signs while screaming at the top of his voice for help.

He wouldn't leave him on the ground to run back inside.

A neighbor heard the commotion.

"Shawn – son, what's going on?"

"It's dad, he's not responding." Without saying a word, the neighbor ran back inside and called 911.

Carol had just turned the shower off when she heard the voice of her son in absolute despair, piercing the air in full panic.

"Daaaaad!"

She snatched a robe and rushed to the window.

George was lying on the ground with one arm outstretched and the other over his stomach, Shawn on one knee standing guard.

Even from a distance she could see her son's eyes Bloody Mary red – fear on his face.

Shaking uncontrollably, Carol sprinted downstairs. She ran out the door, one hand covering her mouth, the other holding the belt around her robe. Carol screamed.

"George!"

CHAPTER NINE: THE CONFRONTATION

The sirens were closing in fast.

The car was still running, the driver side door still open, and the entire Stanley family was on the ground looking at their husband and father. George was not responding.

Neighbors ran out of their houses, jogging frantically across the street while calling Carol's name, hoping for answers, hoping their fears were unfounded.

The ambulance roared around the corner. Help was only seconds away.

"George – George, can you hear me?" Carol asked, her tears spotting her husband's shirt. "George, say something!"

The paramedics rushed up; George's chest began to rise and fall more rapidly.

"What happened?" One of the paramedics asked.
Shawn tried to catch his breath while being as specific as his emotions would allow.

"We were just throwing football; I went inside, looked back out to see my dad still in the driveway, passed out behind the wheel."

"We have to get him to the hospital now." The paramedic said as he wrapped a blood pressure bag around George's arm.

Suddenly, George' chest filled with air and he coughed involuntarily, spitting a mixture of blood and mucous.

"He's coding," The paramedic said.

"Hand me the crash kit!"

Carol let out a high-pitched sound that only accompanies panic.

"He's not breathing," The paramedic said. He ripped open his shirt and began chest compressions while his partner called into the hospital with vital medical data, telling them to be prepared for critical transport.

"One! Two! Three!" The paramedic pressed into

George's chest.

"Oh God – this isn't happening," Shawn mumbled.

Five minutes later, there on the front lawn, George Stanley died, never having made it out of his driveway.

***

The funeral for Mr. George C. Stanley was the following Tuesday. Sitting in the front row of the St. John Parish's church in Austin was Carol, Shawn, friends and family. After hearing of the tragedy, even David Monk and his wife Danielle flew in for the service. The little time Monk spent with George had forged a tie, a tie strong enough to pay his respects in person.

Nothing in the service felt real, because it barely was. How could this have happened? The confusion was as palatable as the event itself. The sobering sense of inevitability that accompanies a long illness wasn't there; it was quite the opposite. Everyone felt that all of this could've been avoided. Dr. Angelo embraced Carol and Shawn as she passed the family to pay respects on her way out of the church, and Gozi came also.

It would be a chance meeting in line as attendees waited to greet the family that allowed for Monk to meet somebody.

"Unbelievable, isn't it?" Monk said to the man in line in front of him.

"It is; I didn't know him, but we share a couple of friends." The man answered.

"I just met him recently at a conference in New York, and he traveled to my office in Ft. Lauderdale to talk about doing business. A great guy – we kinda hit it off right away. I'm just in shock," Monk said

The line was inching closer to the family as each

CHAPTER NINE: THE CONFRONTATION

person took their time to properly greet Carol and reassure his son Shawn that everything would be alright.

"I tell you, it really makes you think about family, and what you're doing with your life. This is a wake-up call for me. I'm dealing with my own health issues, and this only makes me want to be around for my family."

Monk and Danielle were next in line to greet Carol. Monk turned around to shake the man's hand, as they would probably not speak again once both got outside.

"Good speaking with you, what's your name?"

"Stanley George." He responded.

Monk's face flushed.

"Excuse me?"

***

The two men stood outside for an hour discussing what the deceased had been about to do with his money. Stanley revealed he's been in the same place as it relates to his finances. Monk, viewing this as an unbelievable coincidence, offered to pick up with Stanley right where the deceased had left off.

"I'm going to do this at no charge," Monk told Stanley. "I just feel that's the right thing to do. I was going to send George two papers next week on something called "The Future of Money" and "The Losing Game." I'll email them to you tonight and we'll be in touch."

The autopsy for George Stanley revealed he died of an embolism, one that could have been avoided had he gone to the doctor days sooner. If he'd come back from New York, the tests would have shown that he needed to have surgery, possibly saving his life. George operated on the premise he had more time and never felt the pressure of taking care of this issue immediately. But the fact that he didn't know didn't eliminate the consequences of not knowing. The fact that his identity was confused and that he was really the sick one didn't provide mercy from a fast approaching fate. What you don't know can hurt you.

Chapter Ten
THE FUTURE OF MONEY

CHAPTER TEN: THE FUTURE OF MONEY

THE FUTURE OF MONEY IS LESS IMPORTANT than the future of your money. And your decisions today will determine everything. Do you believe in Jesus? Random, isn't it? Came out of nowhere with no connectivity to anything. And right now, as you read this sentence, you're probably saying, "What in the world does this question have to do with investing?" And the answer is, nothing.

One day you will wake up and with no warning, precursor, or blinking indicator lights on your financial dashboard - the dollars in your pocket will be worth little to nothing. This event will come out of nowhere.

You would have gone to bed the night before with all your finances tightly wrapped in a nice little box – your retirement plan in order, money set aside for the unexpected, maybe a vacation home somewhere in the Caribbean and your daughter in graduate school.

When the dollar finally crashes, it will do so overnight. What will you do? What is your backup plan? What can you take to any continent, in the city or back roads of any far land and still get goods and services? The only thing on earth that fits this need is gold. Take the smartest guy on financial television, the pithiest professor at the Wharton School of Business or the most profitable trader on a desk of Goldman Sachs and ask them one question. "You must survive for one year traveling around the globe without access to anyone. What do you want in your pocket? The Yen? The Dollar? The Euro or gold?" Without deviation, each answer will be, "Give me gold." The question is how does one operate on a day-to-day basis using the wisdom of ultimate survival scenarios? You already do. That's why you wear a seatbelt. You treat each drive like an accident is going to occur. Investing should be no different. Gold is that seatbelt.

THE PREMISE, THE MONEY & THE GOLD

***

Nobody talks about September 10th, 2001, but many people were wealthy on the 10th and broke on September 12. This example of an extreme event holds a valuable teaching moment for all investors. On September 12, in London trading, gold spiked from $215.50 to $287 per ounce. Why? Before we answer, think of this. After September 11th, the Federal Reserve added $100 billion in liquidity (paper money) into the US economy to avert a financial crisis. So $100 billion dollars were printed out of the clear blue sky, which means every dollar in existence before this infusion was now worth less. Yet for gold, without any volume being added, or any gold being created, spiked on its own. But even with this evidence, predicting the future of money is still not as simple as the data may make it seem. One still must be careful.

Trying To Predict the Future

Understanding the future of money means understanding far more than economics or high finance; it's about understanding the past, human nature, the human spirit and the cycle of change that seems to come from out of nowhere. And then, even understanding all of that; still be prepared to be wrong.

To predict the future of money, one must first understand what people really want from their money. They want something that lasts, something they can count on, something that will be there when they need it, and something that stands the test of time.

CHAPTER TEN: THE FUTURE OF MONEY

The Need For Certainty Is What Drives Investors.

That is the whole push behind the development of the perfect money system. Investors are constantly seeking certainty in an uncertain and imperfect world, particularly when the market is unstable. They want to know that the chunk of their life they gave away, their body they worked until it hurt, or the sanity they have sacrificed will be worth something in the end and continue to have value, particularly when they are old and no longer able to work.

That is why what is old is new because nobody can come up with anything better than gold or other precious metals as investments that hold value. That means a dollar's worth of gold purchased today will be worth a dollar or more tomorrow instead of 95 cents, 50 cents or even a penny, should the economy turn really bad. Yet at least paper money is cash that can be held until the possibility of a better day. Even bad bank notes are sometimes bought back and their owners can receive something for them. Not so for those who are wealthy 'on paper.' Their wealth can be wiped out in a matter of seconds at the whim of the stock market, leaving them nothing to show for it.

So the question becomes whether gold and precious metals replace stocks and bonds as the first choice for investors and whether this is indeed the future of money.

All That Is Gold Is Not Necessarily Good

Precious metals are not an inherent investment in growth and success; they are a defense against collapse. Gold is not the seaside resort town; it is the plywood that covers the windows in that town so it can weather the storm and open on a future sunny day. As long as the plywood is up, the town is safe, but it's also not making any money. The plywood has to come off the windows, the branches cleaned out of the streets, and the resort needs to be reopened for business.

Stocks, private equity investments, and bonds are the resort. They are representative of things that are dynamic, that are growing. Other than employing miners and gold that is used for industrial applications, investments in gold do not spread through the economy in the same way that investments in stocks fund companies producing consumer goods. That said; the strong presence of gold and other precious metals in the marketplace, and the desire to acquire them, are signs that there are serious structural problems with the market and the overall economy. A healthy market is not searching for security, but opportunity. A scared market is searching for security.

The problem is that the economy is not really in a position to make a turn for the better and begin to generate substantial positive growth in the foreseeable future. There are several reasons for this. Economic and political problems have been developing over the long term and will take time to solve. First and foremost, the economy has shed most of its industrial base and will need to regain some of this before healthy growth can begin.

The next problem is the US is involved in a deep-seated energy crisis that, absent the taking of some significant steps, is just beginning. Thirdly, this country and the world can no longer afford the excesses and wastefulness that brought about our Industrial Revolution. That wastefulness also extends to government spending.

Debt Blocks the Road to Recovery

Another factor that continues to fuel the kind of uncertainty driving investors towards gold and other

CHAPTER TEN: THE FUTURE OF MONEY

precious metals is the level of debt held by the United States Government, which is no longer in a position to spend the nation, and with it the world, out of the current recession. Our current national debt of $15.7 trillion is actually greater than our Gross Domestic Product of $15.2 trillion. In other words, the national debt is 103 percent of GDP. That means the sum of all the products, goods, and services produced by the United States is less than the money the nation owes to its creditors.

In the past, spending by the government has been a traditional road to recovery. At the beginning of the Great Depression, the investment and banking sectors of the economy were in shambles, but the actual economy of the government itself was in pretty good shape. Unlike the current situation, the national debt represented just 4 percent of GDP in 1932. So, President Franklin Roosevelt had the resources he needed to experiment with ways to get the economy going again. All the public works projects stimulated the economy in two ways: they helped put people back to work, which put money in their pockets that they would inevitably spend in the private sector for the necessities of life. And the public works projects became the infrastructure upon which old businesses could expand and new businesses could be built.

Analysts point out that it only worked so well because it took the spending of World War II to pull the nation completely out of the Great Depression. However, economists have shown that the recovery would have been much faster had Roosevelt not chosen to cut spending in the midst of the recovery to placate his foes, causing a double dip downturn.

President Obama tried taking a page from the book of Roosevelt, but the situation now is vastly different. It's not that there's not enough spending in the marketplace; there's too much – from the government. Spending by the government for entitlements and for military commitments around the world that includes the fighting in Afghanistan are sucking money out of the economy that could be used to fund private enterprise. President Obama tried a stimulus package, but it can't stimulate an industrial base that isn't there.

Instead, money is being spent on defense which, like gold and precious metals, does not track through the entire economy. A tank costing an exorbitant sum of money puts defense workers and their suppliers to work, but once it is shipped overseas, the cycle ends. Whereas a car manufactured and sold in the United States continues to stimulate the economy for years after it is manufactured. The dealer will make a profit and will be taxed and spend the profits in the community. The car will need gas, brakes, oil changes, car washes, and everything else associated with maintenance. People around the community will make money from all of that. Plus, the owner will use that car to drive to places that are not easy to reach on foot and shop for groceries, take vacations, etc. All of this comes out of just one car.

Think of the effect of millions of cars or other consumer goods. Until the experts begin to see this, the uncertainty that is the native habitat of gold and precious metals will continue.

Besides the threat of government debt, the pendulum of change has begun to swing in subtle ways that were not evident a few years ago. Talk of protesters used to conjure images of Vietnam War-era hippies or people overseas battling police in riot gear, but that didn't happen here. It's happening now. 'Occupy Wall Street' is a protest movement offering a challenge to the *business as usual* mentality of Wall Street at home, and different 'occupy' movements have sprung up around the country and around the world.

CHAPTER TEN: THE FUTURE OF MONEY

People are angry because they are hurting financially. Nations that accepted without question, the recommendations of the World Bank and the International Monetary Fund in the past, are challenging the 'austerity plans' put forth by those groups. The elected governments of France and Greece agreed to the austerity measures that were part of efforts to reduce debt levels so they could continue to keep the Euro as their currency. Those leaders lost in their respective elections and were replaced by leaders hostile to the austerity measures. The debt levels of many other nations in the Euro zone are also high. Many analysts are wondering if the Euro will be able to remain a viable currency and if it collapses, will it cause the failure of currencies around the world and, with it, bring on a worldwide economic collapse.

If that happens, it will undoubtedly drive gold prices and other precious metals sky high and they will supplant stocks and other securities as the dominant asset in many investor portfolios. The ironic part of the drive to invest in the gold is that the way it's being done defeats the entire purpose of investing in precious metals in the first place – to walk away from the transaction with an object of stable intrinsic value that cannot be lost in the market or to have in hand to use for emergency purchases.

However, that's not much of the gold currently being purchased. *It's virtual gold.*

People and governments, such as China's, are purchasing the gold electronically, but they are not coming to pick it up as many investors did from the United States during the late 1960's and the early 1970's before President Nixon took the nation off the gold standard. People trust the system –and that the gold will be there if they call upon it. Yet, there's nothing to stop these private brokers from going out of business and taking the gold with them or their creditors from seizing it.

Back To the Future Of Money

Not everything is going to happen just because people think it's going to happen based on the current tenor of the times. An amusing scene comes from the first Back to the Future movie, when the 1950's Doc Brown character makes a humorous observation when viewing his future self on the videotape showing him in front of the DeLorean time machine. When he is told the strange clothing he's wearing is a radiation suit, he makes an instant leap that only someone from the 1950's would make: "Of course, because of the fallout from the nuclear wars!"

Everyone burst out in laughter in the theater because it didn't happen in real life. However, to 1950's America, nuclear war wasn't a question of 'if,' but 'when,' because up until the advent of nuclear weapons, every other weapon developed ended up being used in warfare. There was no reason for 1950's Americans to believe that it wouldn't be any different than the rest of history.

It was an easy leap to make given the tenor of the times, but it was completely wrong. Right now, there are a lot of scary prospects on the horizon concerning the future of money. The increasing investment in gold is not a positive sign, but a negative one. The economy does have serious structural problems. An energy crisis is looming over the entire world. The resource base of the planet is being used up at stupendous rate. The extreme debt of the government of the United States threatens to topple the world's financial system. Protesters could increase to the point of radically changing the entire system. However, just because it looks like something is going to happen doesn't mean it's going to happen.

Things can change and the situation could be pulled back from the abyss. Some unforeseen or unforeseeable factor could kick in that, in retrospect, makes this whole argument seem silly. The bottom line is nobody knows, but we do know that gold protects you no matter what. It's like water; no matter what happens in the world, you're going to need it.

Chapter Eleven
THE LOSING GAME

CHAPTER ELEVEN: THE LOSING GAME

LOSING IS INFECTIOUS BECAUSE IT'S EASY TO DUPLICATE. Losing is like the common cold; everyone can catch it. Losing provides a kind of cultural attachment, a bond with the average man. It is a sickening bond, but a bond nonetheless. But even more damaging is the pattern a losing mentality creates. Normalized losing is a phenomenon of human behavior. You've probably noticed over the last twenty years how the losing mindset is everywhere. For example, have you noticed how Little League sports now concentrates on 'good efforts' instead of winning? And how the excuse for this is: 'to build confidence and appreciate the efforts of trying.'

And this is to be a life skill? Parents accept this concept because they accept losing, but how many times will your child be rewarded for going on a job interview? Never. 'Life skills' is knowing how to win – yes, winning fairly, but winning. No child ever paid a bill by simply 'trying hard.' The next time you need to pay a mortgage note, call the bank and tell them, "I tried" and see what the response is. It will be something like, "our foreclosure depart is 'trying' right now to serve you with papers."

This is said with some humor, but there is a more profound point here for all of us, that is, to change our mentality to that which *rewards* and not simply *attempts*. But as an investor, Wall Street wants you to expect to lose. They want losing to be normalized in your life. This lowers the standards of performance on their part.

Investor profiling

Investor profiling assumes all investors are the same. As we've discovered, even if you and another investor have similar names, are from the same place and have similar interests, our investment solutions would still be night and day in terms of their differences. It's difficult to step outside of the plaster mold poured for every American investor, but you must do it; your future and that of your family depends on it. Don't take another person's medicine and don't take investment advice not designed for you. Never take for granted that the individual paid to help you *will help you*. Get used to the counter-intuition needed to change your life. This requires that you fundamentally see yourself differently than you ever have. It requires you rid yourself of false premise so your mistakes don't compound into greater consequences.

Seeing yourself differently causes everyone looking at you to see you differently. Seeing yourself differently surfaces rights and privileges not offered to the common man. Right or wrong, it's just the way it is. Options that are beyond the status quo are only presented to those who understand there's more to offer and to gain. It's like the time you walked into a store and asked for the 20% discount. And then when you walked out of the door, you wondered, if you didn't mention the discount, would it have been offered to you? Probably not.

And so it is with investing; if you don't know, it won't be told to you. If you don't seek better information, you will receive that which is acceptable to the masses. If you don't demand that gold and other precious metals be a part of your long term investment strategy, it will not be. And you will hear every excuse in the world why it isn't right for you. It will all make sense as long as you don't think about it. Investing in gold is like betting it will rain in Hilo, Hawaii, where it rains, on average, over 270 days per year. You may find a guy in Yuma, Arizona, where it only rains on average 17 days a year, tell you how betting on rain is a terrible investment, and that would be the case if you were betting on Yuma, but you're betting on Hilo.

CHAPTER ELEVEN: THE LOSING GAME

Wall Street and many financial advisors make global proclamations for what only has local applications. You have to make decisions for where you are, not where somebody else is. Advising investors not to put their money in gold is assuming everyone is in the same place, has the same needs, and the same future. It is investor profiling at its worse.

Investing *well* is investing in what should work for *you*. Concentrate on *you*, because when you need money at 78, you can bet your life that the advisor, who advised you to stay out of gold, will not write you a check to cover the effects of his bad advice.

Investing well is so often missed because it has little to do with investing. Making money has little to do with making money, and success has little to do with trying to be successful. Instead, all of these sought after objectives have everything to do with mindset, thus premise, thus who is controlling our fundamental concepts.

Why is it that some people seem to get it and others don't? It is because getting 'it' is really a function of getting yourself. This is why money is tagged as an intellectual sport . . . not intellect as it relates to academic achievement, but rather elegant reasoning abilities based on raw facts of human nature.

People with money are people. They aren't a higher species or aliens. All billionaires labor on the toilet; whether the toilet be faced with 18k gold, or Exxon side of the road nasty, they're all sitting on it at some point in the day. Never forget that.

How does this help? It helps because it reveals the equity of opportunity. It establishes proper premise. It lets you know your ideas are as valid as anyone's. What is Buffett doing that I'm not doing? Even if you figured out one-half of one percent, you'd be rich. But most people will never even take the time to process this thought. Most would rather fall in line and obey the rules, but blindly following what you've been told to believe can have eternal consequences.

The word "consequences" conjures a negative connotation. In very practical terms, it means to experience a sequence of events that runs contrary to your desired path. Thus, the consequences or sequence of events after stepping in front of a truck are usually bad.

Bad premise not only creates bad approaches to problems that don't really exist but even after we've solved the problem for ourselves, it can live on in the lives of others. The wealthiest families on earth were not the wealthiest families two hundred years ago. The generation that now exists, lives in the wake of good decisions made by their forefathers, decisions that were based on accurate premise and solid reasoning. Making better decisions for your money, investing in that which everyone but the entity with the most money, government, discourages, and establishing a path towards independent thinking can do more than save your financial future; it can save your life.

***

This year Thanksgiving would be held at Stanley and Nicole's house. Family was traveling in from all over the country, many they hadn't seen in years. Nicole finally got the extra room added on; the library and basement were now fully appointed. This year, both in-laws would be there, and even Uncle Joe was invited.

Stanley's account, although not what it was in 2006, had stabilized and edged up a solid 20% from the day he cashed out with Barry and invested with David Monk. Monk

CHAPTER ELEVEN: THE LOSING GAME

had changed his life for the better. Without Monk, and the unique way in which their lives crossed, Stan wouldn't have had the confidence to do what he did.

"I'll never forget those words," Stan often recalls of a pivotal conversation with Monk. "Don't risk what you have and need for what you don't have and don't need." It was a phrase Monk borrowed from Warren Buffett, and it just stuck. Friends who had lost homes, boats, and businesses were now all interested in gold. Everyone wanted to know how Stan had recovered and gained in a market where losing had become normalized.

Smells and sounds of holiday joy filled the air, breads, casseroles, laughter and good will. Family and close friends sat around the table, not an inch of available space. This was tradition, but today, tradition made Stan reflect on how thankful he really was. His family was here to celebrate the holiday - show their support and love. Everyone had been through a lot when they thought Stan only had a short time. Now that they knew differently, it was time to enjoy life.

The atmosphere was thick with appreciation, and to think he was going to end his life, for no reason. Today, he was a client of Monk and his finances were better than they'd ever been in his life.

In the kitchen, Nicole was working on the last dishes for the meal. She'd cooked a large turkey, as well as a ham, and had a spread of mashed potatoes, potatoes au gratin, stuffing, cranberry sauce, at least five types of salad, and grilled vegetables. She was an amazing cook, and it all smelled wonderful.

Stan turned to his wife, leaned over and whispered in her ear.

"I invited Carol."

Both looked at each other with an understanding only eyes could express. Just then, Uncle Joe raised his glass.

"Attention, attention!"

Nicole leaned over and whispered back in Stan's ear. "I hope she and Shawn show up."

Uncle Joe focused the table's concentration.

"Let's toast to a healthy man, a good man, my nephew and friend, Stanley and his beautiful wife Nicole.

"Hear, hear!" the table shouted as glasses touched with the familiar tingle.

Several minutes went by. The table quieted a bit. Nicole noticed something didn't feel right.

"Stan - where's Jesse?" she asked

"Not sure; she's probably playing with her cousins."

"Can you go find her?"

Stan didn't see the rush, but got up anyway and hustled upstairs to her room grunting all the way.

"Knock, knock, knock!"

"Kids, you guys ok?"

Stan pushed the door open slowly to see inside. The cousins were all playing video games and board games. One group was playing hide and seek, and another coloring on the learning table - but Jesse wasn't there.

"Hey, guys, where's Jesse?"

"She ran downstairs."

"Really? How long ago?" Stan asked

"About ten minutes, Uncle Stan," one niece answered.

Stan went back downstairs and peeked round the corner into Jesse's favorite spot in the house, the reading room where she always cuddled up next to him while Stan read for hours. He'd had a smaller chair built just for her, so that she could sit on her own and feel grown up. She'd used it once and never again. She preferred to sit on the arm of the chair where he was sitting, or – even better – in his lap, leaning back against him so she could see the books as well. She loved the picture

CHAPTER ELEVEN: THE LOSING GAME

books, of course, but she was equally attracted to the more adult books on engineering and money. She would stare at pages and pages of diagrams and text as he read. He swore that this had led to her learning to read earlier than most kids. Part of it had probably been memorization – remembering what words went where in the books she insisted on reading again and again.

Jesse would usually fall asleep right there and Stan would carry her upstairs to her room in the middle of the night. These days, she was starting to read some of the passages herself. Only in the simpler books, of course, though she had insisted the other day that they start moving on to more advanced stuff. Incredibly smart girl, he thought to himself. She was going to go far in life; he could feel it. She had the drive and intelligence to do so, and that sunny personality. She just didn't understand the word 'no.' Nor, he suspected, would she understand the idea of giving up. Jesse was a classic 'never say die' girl. His girl, his life.

Stan's thoughts raced back to the scene in his office months before, when he'd forgotten about how much his family meant to him for only a few seconds, a very dangerous few seconds. It wasn't like him, and the fact that he'd gone that far at all still bothered him. He was lucky he'd heard Jesse coming when he did. Lucky he'd been able to get the gun back in the drawer. If she'd seen him, there would have been questions, misunderstandings. Thank God, he'd heard her.

Stan's thoughts came back to the task at hand, finding his little spider, Jesse was probably hiding under a couch somewhere. Her books and his were scattered all around the floor, *Goodnight Moon* and *Economics in One Lesson* touched on the floor. Dr. Seuss and *Wealth of the Nations* on top of one another. The mixture of children's books and adult material seemed especially poignant right now – the dependence of the one on the other, the combination of mature material with the innocence of youth. Toys and teddy bears mixed with stock charts and scribblings; in Stan's eyes the most beautiful site. It symbolized his love for his daughter, and the way she looked up to him. She'd been coming to his office since she could walk, asking what he was doing, interested in learning more about the simplest things – how to use a calculator, how to fill out a check. This combination of toys and stock charts seem to be a physical sign of Jesse. But where was Jesse, he began to worry just a little.

Stan turned back toward the kitchen, frowning, and met his wife's eyes. It wasn't like their daughter to disappear without any explanation. She usually announced where she was going – and why – to the entire world.

Nicole pulled away from the table and meet Stan in the reading room. She took one look at his face and grew concerned herself.

"I can't find her down here, and I've looked everywhere," she told him. "She's not upstairs?"

"No," he answered, "Nothing in our reading spot either. Books and toys spread all over the place, but no sign of her. Looks like she left in a rush, wherever she's gone."

Nicole's frown became deeper, but she closed her eyes and took a deep breath. "Well, let's not panic. I'm sure she's here somewhere, and us getting upset will only frighten her. Have you tried actually calling her? Maybe she's hiding somewhere, playing some sort of game."

Stan snorted. That would, after all, be like his daughter. She was always making up games without telling her parents the rules. It had led to a number of confusing situations, as Stan and Nicole found that they were breaking rules without even realizing it, and losing games they didn't know they were playing. If she was hiding somewhere…

CHAPTER ELEVEN: THE LOSING GAME

"Jesse! Jesse?" he called. There was no response, and he began to walk slowly through the house. "Honey, I know you may be playing a game right now, but we need you to come out and talk to us."

As he walked through the rooms, he found additional signs of quick movement from his daughter. A discarded sweater here, one of her hair ribbons there. He even found one of her shoes in the corner of the dining room. There was no sign of the little girl, though, and he could feel his heart starting to constrict with worry. He'd promised Nicole that he wouldn't freak out, but it was getting harder by the moment. Where was his daughter? Why wasn't she responding to his voice? She always came when he called her! Where had she been going in such a hurry, and why had it necessitated eliminated one shoe, a hair ribbon, and her sweater?

Now he couldn't remember the last time he'd seen Jesse. He'd locked that drawer, hadn't he? Surely he had – there was an automatic lock on the drawer, and it snapped shut as soon as the drawer rolled closed. Still, he had to check. She spent a lot of time in his office. He rushed toward the stairs in a full sprint, his breathing now heavy. He glanced out the window to see several of the kids from the neighborhood playing. He opened the back door and called out to them. They hadn't.

"Have you seen Jesse?" Stan asked one of his nephews as he ran by.

"No, Uncle Stan," the boy responded, shaking his head. "Is she missing?"

Stan nodded, a bit dazed, and glanced around the room. "Yeah, I don't know when the last time I saw her was, and I'm just wondering where she got off to. I don't want to worry anyone, but can you ask your cousins to help us look? Just let them know she might be hiding somewhere, playing some sort of game. I don't want her to get upset about us searching for her. I just want to find her."

The boy nodded and ran toward the playroom, shouting for his cousins. Stan began to get a more concerned, his anxiety rising as there were few places left where she could be. Nicole ran up behind Stan outside.

"Is she out here?"

"No."

Nicole bit her lip, her eyes spanning across the room and coming back to her husband. "Where on earth could she be?" she asked, her voice colored with growing fear. "I don't think she's playing a game. At least not any kind of game I know. She couldn't have gotten out of the house, could she? She wouldn't have left without us, I can't imagine that."

She paused and looked down, then looked back up at Stan, her eyes wide and teary. "Oh God, Stan, you don't suppose someone came in here and took her?"

He swallowed hard. He hadn't had that precise thought, but now that she said it out loud, he realized it was close to what he'd been thinking. He shook his head, though, not wanting to upset Nicole.

"I'm sure she's here somewhere. We just have to find her. Come on, let's get everyone involved. If Jesse *is* playing a game, she'll love it if everyone else joins in."

Both ran back inside as what had been a little concern began to morph into something more serious. Stan walked hurriedly by the dinner table where as yet, no one was aware of his and Nicole's inability to locate Jesse. He shouted over the conversations as he appeared and then disappeared into the kitchen.

"Has anyone seen Jesse?" he shouted, looking around the room. He prayed that everyone would see how concerned he was and take him seriously. Some of his family members

CHAPTER ELEVEN: THE LOSING GAME

had a tendency to joke too often, and too many of them wrote off his love for his daughter. He needed them to be serious this time, though, or he might start shouting.

For once, everyone did what he needed them to do. The dialogue dropped off as several family members and friends pushed back from the table to join in the search. The moment Stan entered the kitchen again, he noticed something odd.

He'd just remembered his original suspicion. His office. The door leading to the basement – it was ajar. He kept that door locked at all times but had rushed to answer the front door when family started arriving earlier in the day. He'd mistakenly left the key in the door knob. He swung the door open wide and yelled downstairs.

"Jesse, are you down here!"

No answer to his question but he heard something in the distance, someone was counting.

"One, Ninety, Seven."

Jesse was opening his top drawer.

"Oh God" Stan mumbled as he ran down the stairs leaping over the last three steps. He tripped and slammed against the leg of the couch.

From the floor, he looked up and screamed in horror. "Jesse!"

Jesse looked up.

"I want to be just like you daddy."

***

In reading this story, undoubtedly, several ideas have surfaced in your mind. Let us hear the conclusion of the whole matter. Every action is based on some piece of information gathered from somebody, somewhere, at some period of time. This makes it critical to examine who influences us, and who we influence. Our decisions go far beyond money; our decisions affect the lives of those who observe the decisions we make. And that's where it gets tricky. Something that we correct in our own lives may remain uncorrected in the lives of those who observed us. And that is why premise is so critical, there's so much at stake, but good decisions can be just as influential as bad ones.

Take this book, give it to a friend, give it to an enemy. Each will come to their own conclusion about what happened to Jesse, and if you read this book again, your opinion may change also as you see things you didn't at first see.

THE END

ACKNOWLEDGMENTS

The road to writing my first book has been long, but rewarding. So many people have contributed to accomplishing the goal you now hold in your hands. First and foremost, I want to thank my wife Danielle for being a living example of how beautiful life can be. She inspires me to never settle for less than excellence. I want to thank my failures for motivating me to prove to myself that I could not only chase my dreams, but one day catch them. There are numerous family and friends who have made substantial contributions to my life - you know exactly who you are, I sincerely thank you. And to Dennis Ross, III for opening that secret portal called 'great writing,' and encouraging me to take on this journey without hesitation.

Notes

http://www.coinsite.com/content/articles/Confederational.asp

http://en.wikipedia.org/wiki/Early_American_currency

http://www.thebhc.org/publications/BEHprint/v013/p0159-p0170.pdf

http://www.philadelphiafed.org/education/teachers/resources/money-in-colonial-times/

http://www.enotes.com/national-bank-act-1864-reference/national-bank-act-1864

http://en.wikipedia.org/wiki/Necessary_and_Proper_Clause

http://www.coin-collecting-guide-for-beginners.com/quarter-eagle.html

http://www.coins.nd.edu/ColCurrency/CurrencyIntros/IntroValue.html

http://wiki.answers.com/Q/Why_did_the_articles_of_confederation_not_allow_the_stats_to_coin_their_own_money

http://www.famguardian.org/Subjects/MoneyBanking/FederalReserve/FRconspire/private.htm

http://en.wikipedia.org/wiki/United_States_Note

http://mises.org/Community/forums/t/7052.aspx

http://en.wikipedia.org/wiki/National_Bank_Act

http://en.wikipedia.org/wiki/History_of_the_United_States_dollar

http://www.pbs.org/newshour/businessdesk/2012/04/does-the-fed-create-money-out.html

http://www.globalresearch.ca/index.php?context=va&aid=10489

http://www.federalreserve.gov/aboutthefed/bios/board/default.htm

http://en.wikipedia.org/wiki/List_of_countries_by_population

David S. Bogen, *The Scandal of Smith and Buchanan: The Skeletons in the McCulloch vs. Maryland Closet,* University of Maryland Law School Digital Commons

http://digitalcommons.law.umaryland.edu/cgi/viewcontent.cgi?article=1251&context=fac_pubs&sei-redir=1.

Richard W. Painter, *Ethics and Corruption in Business and Government: Lessons From the South Sea Bubble and the Bank of the United States,* University of Minnesota Law School Legal Studies Research Paper Series Research Paper No. 06-32

http://www.scribd.com/doc/27621954/Ethics-and-Corruption-in-Business-and-Government.

David Cowen, "The First Bank of the United States," EH.net, Economic History Association, http://eh.net/encyclopedia/article/cowen.banking.first_bank.us.

"The Second Bank of the United States: A Chapter in the History of Central Banking," Federal Reserve Bank of Philadelphia. http://www.philadelphiafed.org/publications/economic-education/second-bank.pdf.

David Kinley, *The History, Organization, and Influence of the Independent Treasury* (New York: Thomas Y. Crowell, 1893), 25, 35, 38.

Orville Marcellus Powers, *Commerce and Finance,* (Chicago: Powers & Lyons, 1903), 254.